Huckleberry Days

A Time That Was And Is No More

George L. Hand

iUniverse, Inc.
New York   Bloomington

Huckleberry Days
A Time That Was And Is No More

iUniverse books may be ordered through booksellers or by contacting:

iUniverse
1663 Liberty Drive
Bloomington, IN 47403
www.iuniverse.com
1-800-Authors (1-800-288-4677)

Because of the dynamic nature of the Internet, any Web addresses or links contained in this book may have changed since publication and may no longer be valid.

ISBN: 978-1-4401-9631-7 (sc)
ISBN: 978-1-4401-9630-0 (ebk)

Printed in the United States of America

iUniverse rev. date: 11/24/2009

Contents

Introduction

These stories for you are all the truth,
From years ago in Grandpa's youth.
Life was great for boys back then.
Boys not teens but at least ten.
We're old enough to come and go.
Our folks thought that this should be so.
In fact most moms would say to one,
"Get out doors in the fresh air and sun.
"Be back by lunch or dinner please."
Or before dark in the summer eves.
This was before electronic instruments.
We had to invent our own amusements.
No TV, no computers, no electronic stuff.
We had our wits and that's enough.

1. A Great Place For Boys

We lived by field and orchard and wood.
The greatest place for boys- it was good.
Across from us, next door, and out behind
Was space for anything we had in mind.
I could go forth from house out back,
And walk four miles on path and track.
There were old farms and water company land,
Plus county park, it was wild though planned.
Only one road crossed this wonderful place.
Who'd expect so much near an urban space?
There was water for fishing and winter fun,
But not for swimming, it wasn't done.
Brooks drained swamp and nearby pond.
Of trees and vines we were always fond.
Nearby orchards were old with knobby fruit,
Which none would eat, it didn't suit.
Birds perch on these tree limbs to rest,
And many leave treasure of what's best.
They've eaten berries from here and there.
Thus, our orchards have new fruit to bear.
We picked berries and nuts- all free.
There was even a rare persimmon tree.
But movies and stores were also near,
So we didn't miss out there- don't fear.
We had one advantage that was so great,
Walking everywhere was our fate.

2. The Brook

Something about a rushing stream
Attracts a boy not yet a teen.
A place to build a dam from rocks
After taking off his shoes and socks.
Were the pool bigger, he could swim,
But wading will be enough for him.
Now and then he'll spot a crawdad.
Can he catch it, this brave lad?
They can pinch. You must take care.
Too late, it's scooted to its lair.
He can launch a ship or two,
Any piece of wood will do.
Then try to hit it with a stone,
Or splash his friend, if not alone.
It's time to go, how time has flown.
Should he wreck the dam for play?
No, let it stay for another day,
Or another kid who comes this way.

3. Walking

Walking was the way to go for us.
We'd never ask Dad, and there was no bus.
Mom didn't drive, we had only one car.
Kids didn't mind no matter how far.
Besides, for part of the years of war,
The car was garaged on blocks off the floor.
Our grammar school was less than a half mile,
And the road only went uphill for a while.
At noon we came home for lunch each day,
So we got our exercise in the normal way.
The road's a mile to the ice cream store,
While the movie up town was a bit more.
We walked to skate, we walked to fish,
We walked wherever, whatever our wish.
This was no hardship for us you see.
It just was the way that life ought to be.
Kids were able to sit still in schools.
No drugs needed, and we followed the rules.

4. The Games

Summer was the time for outdoor fun.
In the evenings we surely had enough sun.
Having a neighborhood with kids galore,
Younger and older, both boy and girl.
Out front in the street, we often played ball,
Though a walk to the grammar school was no trouble at all.
Equal teams were chosen each day,
And whoever was there got to play.
Each team would have four, five or more.
I'm not even sure how well we kept score.
Arguments always occurred, "I'm safe," "You're out."
Our games were less about skill and more about shout.
The organizer of most games was Connie next door.
Starting ball games or hide-and-seek was no chore.
Connie was older, a girl most mature.
Was she practicing motherhood? I'm not sure.
When I was older, on this fact I'd reflect.
The neighborhood organizer has a great effect.
An older girl like Connie I'd always select.

5. Going to Work

Going to work with a parent is not something new.
We did it back then, it was a good thing to do.
Dad was a letter carrier, but I must explain more.
You shouldn't say mailman, or he'd be pretty sore.
His day started early with the sorting of mail
For the route he'd deliver on foot without fail.
A truck took mail bundles for boxes along the route.
Dad would visit them and take each one out.
That way he didn't have to carry the whole load.
The work was hard enough, you may have been told.
Kids weren't supposed to be anywhere about,
So I'd meet him outside at the start of the route.
We'd walk and we'd talk, and I'd deliver some mail,
And we'd stop for coffee or rest without fail.
The postal patrons liked my Dad a lot.
Some provided refreshments especially when hot.
I learned much from my Dad in those past days.
Treat people with kind respect in all ways.
You may not have the greatest job around,
But people will see you as a gem that they've found.

6. The Copshoot

There's a place where the cops shot their guns.
This provided a special place for our fun.
We called it the copshoot for want of a name.
Maybe other people called it the same.
To get there, first walk behind the school,
Then follow the brook to where it pools.
We could just as well go by street,
But the woods way was hard to beat.
We went there when it was not in use.
I'm sure they'd chase us with no excuse.
Our mission was to find some lead.
It was great for melting. There was no dread.
We didn't know how poisonous lead could be.
We handled it and played with it rather casually.
First we searched where targets were mounted,
But some of the shooters, their bullets counted.
They recast the slugs for another time.
They weren't opposed to saving a dime.
We discovered another spot quite by chance
In the wood beyond the targets amongst the plants.
We found a spent bullet here and there.
Some of the shots were wild without compare.
Our jean pockets stuffed with the lead weight,
We headed home, so as not to be late.
In the fireplace down stairs, I melted my lead.
I used an old pot on coals in a bed.
I never used the lead in molding a toy.
The fun was the treasure hunting for joy.
Later I sold some for the war to employ.

7. The Railroad Tracks

Out beyond the copshoot lay the track.
However, of railroad trains, there was a lack.
It served two lumber mills and a stone quarry.
Not a very active track, but that's the story.
We'd walk the tracks, it was our pleasure.
Maybe we'd find a railroad spike as treasure.
Anyone who's walked the tracks will know,
It's hard to walk fast, and hard to walk slow.
You have to take baby steps or a long stride,
Since the ties are spaced a little too wide.
Sometimes we'd put something on the rail.
A penny was good or something as frail.
The idea was to return at a later date,
To see what was the penny's fate.
We never found a coin that we had left.
We did find other's coins. This was not theft.
Some kids put small logs on the track.
Not a good idea, but it couldn't cause a wreck.
These trains moved a bit faster than a walk,
And anything like this wouldn't cause a balk.
We knew enough to get off the tracks. We're sane.
But it didn't matter since we never met a train.

8. Laughing

I went over to visit my buddy one day.
Three of us decided to meet for play.
I guess I should say like a modern lout,
That we were going over just to hang out.
In the empty garage, we were fooling around.
The car was gone, but plenty of junk was to be found.
One did something that hit the funny bone.
We laughed a bit. It's more funny when not alone.
Laughter is strange, since you catch the feeling.
It kept us going until we were reeling.
Whatever was done turned out to be funny.
We laughed until our eyes and our noses were runny.
Finally, we stopped when our ribs hurt a bit.
Enough for one day of our laughing fit.
We agreed to meet again the very next day,
But somehow it didn't work out that way.
Spontaneous is one thing, but planned doesn't work.
When each acted silly, he just felt like a jerk.
Maybe our wild time was just a quirk.

9. Skating

We liked winter back in the day.
It meant skating, sledding, cold weather play.
We had four spots nearby to skate.
Sayer's pond behind the school was great.
No fishing, no swimming, was the ruling,
But skating was allowed- no fooling.
Next to the pond were dreary bogs,
All filled with trees and downed logs.
We loved to skate among this litter,
And tag was harder there but better.
Of course, if you broke through- bad luck.
You were wet and cold and smelled of muck.
Always big kids had their fires warm,
So falling in really did no harm.
We raced, played tag, and crack-the-whip,
And jumped for distance trying not to trip.
Some figure skated making their eights,
For this, one needed special skates.
Younger kids counted times that they went down.
We hit the ice a lot, but with no frown.
Hockey the game we did not play.
Just as well- no equipment in the day.
Now kids don't skate on natural ice.
Only Zamboni smooth will suffice.

10. The Little Pond

The little pond was down the street.
We skated there after snow or sleet.
It was easier to clear, though fairly small.
Pushing snow by shovel- do not fall.
One time we piled the snow up high,
In the center- it grew by and by.
We skated in circles so fast around it,
Then someone thought an idea that fit.
Let's collect all the Christmas trees,
And pile them there, if you please.
Later we had a bonfire bright.
We enjoyed skating in the glow at night.
Our parents when they thought about it,
Figured we'd be alright, no doubt about it.

11. Sledding

Behind our school there was a slope.
For snow and sledding we'd surely hope.
Our teachers and principal, the greatest kind,
Let us bring our sleds to school- no mind.
The best snow was wet from a day in the sun.
It packed slippery nice and made a good run.
Sometimes we sat and steered with our feet.
This way two could ride with enough seat.
But if you wanted to get the most speed,
You ran and did a belly flop, we agreed.
Some may feel careening down a hill,
Going head first is too much of a thrill.
If you were smart, you had a short rope,
So you could pull your sled back up the slope.
The other choice was to carry the sled.
It was heavy with iron and wood- like lead.
Some kids, it seems, couldn't steer so well,
And cut down those trudging back up the hill.
There was enough to go wrong in retrospect,
With our sleds and our ways, like having a wreck.
But we never thought of danger then,
For what we did was too much fun.
I saved two sleds down over the years,
For my kids and grand kids and their peers,
But none have used them due to fears,
Of cuts and bruises and maybe worse,
And I guess this feeling I must endorse.
So the sleds were junked with some remorse.

12. Snowball Fights

When the snow has melted and is just right,
You can make good snowballs and have a fight.
New fallen snow is usually too dry.
It won't pack together however you try.
The good kind of snow's for snowman and fort,
For battles between teams, a type of a sport.
The kids pack up snowballs in a big clump.
Each fort would have its own ammo dump.
The best kind of battle has one team attack.
The defenders have better targets when firing back.
Occasionally, the guys would gang up on one,
And pummel him mercilessly until he'd run.
Unfair tactics like these would make you mad,
And cancel out all the fun you've had.
Sometimes an older girl would be the foe,
And she'd wash someone's face with snow.
An unfair tactic was a ball of ice.
I got a bloody mouth once from this device.
We never threw snowballs at our school.
This was against the school time rule.
They even announced that coming or going,
There would not be any snowball throwing.
Now if kids had a snowball fight,
The adults would make them do it right,
And wear helmets with face guards put on tight.

13. Suicide Sledding

The road went up the hill for a mile.
We trudged all the way for a sledding trial.
The trip was a hike. The road was plowed.
They used no salt. Sledding's allowed.
At least no one said that it was not.
There were a few cars though not a lot.
We got to the top and made up our minds.
We'd go down the far side. What would we find?
A car went ahead, so we'd wait a bit.
It wouldn't do to run into it.
Then we did our run, one at a time,
And zipped on down without reason or rhyme.
Then after a curve, that car was ahead.
We had not waited enough time, we said.
So each on the left we passed with speed.
There wasn't much choice, we later agreed.
Whew, that was a close one. We continued on down,
And got to the bottom with no public renown.
Finally, after a pretty long run,
We trudged up the hill for still more fun.
Going toward home would be our last slide.
We wouldn't be as fast going down this side.
We'd forgotten bare pavement partway to town.
Hang on tight 'cause the sled'll surely slow down.
Going faster than sled is not good form.
Your body on pavement will get kinda warm.
A shower of sparks did spray out behind.
We both stayed on board, so we didn't mind.
We survived our wild slides on that day,
Though the sled's steel runners had worn away,
But were still good enough for more winter play.

14. Vines

We walked into the woods one day,
And stopped for a rest along the way.
We had not noticed this special spot,
Though we'd passed nearby a lot.
There were wild grape vines growing free.
That is, away from the trunk of the tree.
How did the vines grow up there?
They couldn't support themselves on air.
They must have grown as the tree grew,
The lower limbs dying as they do.
Being kids with active minds,
We thought of Tarzan swinging on vines.
He could travel from tree to tree,
Though his vines looked like rope to me.
We cut the vine down by its base.
The ground was sloping at this place.
Walk up a way and hang on tight.
Launch into the air. It's almost like flight.
Vine and boy trace a great arc.
Can anything be better than this lark?
Then we thought of something fine.
Swing out on one, then grab another vine.
Do it wrong and drop to the ground.
You can only gasp with no other sound,
This is how the wind's knocked out.
"I'm all right," I could finally shout.
And I'll be ready to swing apace,
When we return to our special place.

15. Birches

When I was young, we could be free.
If we'd the urge, we'd climb a tree.
Boys will be boys was the philosophy.
We could be all we're meant to be.
I'm sure someone could break an arm,
Though I knew none who were so harmed.
My Dad told me about swinging ways,
Not a famous poet from bygone days.
How to pick a birch that was just right,
That one could climb before taking flight.
It must be flexible with narrow girth,
Elsewise, it won't bend down to earth.
Birch trees are found at edge of wood.
In ice storms they'd bend and so were good.
Birch limbs are rare close to the ground.
We had to shinny, legs and arms around.
When high enough, it felt just right,
Launch feet in space, but hold on tight.
If judgement was good, the tree bent so,
The boy would wind up down below.
Let go and drop the last small gap.
If you're too low, it's like a trap.
Go higher still, go hand over hand,
Then the birch should bent toward land.
This is how we made our marks,
When we built our own amusement parks.

16. The Pines

The pine trees were out beyond the field.
They were planted to increase the water yield.
The town water company owned the land.
They didn't mind kids playing in their stand.
There were two types of needles, soft and hard.
We liked this place. The trees we never marred.
Later we found the soft pines were white,
While the hard were red if we got that right.
These trees were not that tall we found.
They still had many limbs down near the ground.
This made great hideouts from other kids.
When we played our games, it's where we hid.
Also, we thought if we were lost in the snow,
This would be a good place for us to go.
But as the trees grow, themselves they shade.
The lower limbs die. It becomes more like a glade.
This happened here, but after we'd grown.
Younger generations stayed away from this zone.
They never knew of the fun that we'd known.

17. Horseback

The farmers stopped farming before my birth,
But one up the street still had some worth.
The barn was still there as sturdy as ever.
They rented out space for horses. It was clever.
People paid for a stall and oats and some hay.
The horses were happy at night and by day.
They were rented per hour for riding in woods,
Which we did with gusto whenever we could.
By could, I mean able to get up the cash.
One fifty per hour, in those days was rash.
We always found ways our money to earn.
I worked in the greenhouse amongst flower and fern.
Mostly, I was careful the way it was spent,
But riding those horses, that's where it went.
There were English and western saddles to choose.
Western for us with no balance to lose.
We knew the horn is used when roping steer,
But it provided a handle for novices, don't sneer.
We rode out the many bridal trails
That crossed the woods for many miles.
"No Galloping," said signs along the way,
But we ignored them, once to my dismay.
We hollered "Hi ho, Silver," and "Giddy up, Scout,"
My horse was spooked by this loud shout.
He stopped short, but I did not,
Continuing forward like a shot.
We wore no helmets, this is true,
And the result of this I could rue.
But the trail was soft with churned up dust,
And with but a jar, I ended my thrust.
We know God guards both fool and drunk,
But maybe also boys with some spunk.

18. Woods Fires

Now and then in the land out back,
The fields or woods had a fire attack.
I may sound cavalier about this now,
But these didn't endanger much, I vow.
They cleared out litter and dense cat briar,
Which had no control in woods except fire.
No house was ever threatened nor barn,
Nor any big tree by fire was harmed.
When the siren sounded kids came on the run.
They wanted to help and so have great fun.
An Indian pump, the big boys hoped to acquire,
A man's job to help put out that fire.
The pumps were heavy and worn as a pack.
The lesser flames they're used to attack.
You may wonder why they'd want this prize.
It was mostly for bragging rights amongst the guys.
But how did the fires start out there in the wood?
I know about one as you expect I would.
My buddy and I had matches that day.
We wanted to start a fire for play.
Just a small one in the field on a path.
All the dry straw didn't compute in our math.
The fire did spread, and we did stamp.
It would have been nice if it were more damp.
The best thing then for us was to run,
And we figured out that we'd tell no one.
This often happens when there is trouble.
Kids run away, then the problem may double.
So say to your kids, "Tell us what's true,
"And then we'll never punish you."

19. Smoking

We know that smoking is pretty bad,
So don't think poorly of my Dad.
We had gone fishing. The mosquitos were wild.
Dad gave me a weed though I was only a child.
The smoke was supposed to keep them away.
I'm still not sure if it's true what they say.
This started me smoking, but I never bought any,
Since my friend Bill's Dad had so many.
Cigarettes, cigars, and supplies for his pipe,
Were all over their house for us to swipe.
And the old guy never missed any of it,
Though we didn't smoke enough to make it a habit.
In later years I've read that teens,
Could become addicted to smokes by easy means.
This problem stopped with a very odd cure.
Bill moved away, and smoking lost its allure.
Strangely enough, I knew as a lad
That for our health, cigarettes are certainly bad.
Cancer sticks and coffin nails were names they had.

20. The Bike

On reaching twelve I had some luck.
I bought my cousin's bike for seven bucks.
It didn't look like much, it was old,
But I didn't care since I was bold.
I'd get it running and paint it red,
And then I'd have some wheels, I said.
With effort I got the bike working one day.
I learned by trial and error along the way.
And then I had to learn to ride.
It's something that I'd never tried.
When you're young is the time to learn.
Kids seem better with balance, pump, and turn.
My experience started on our lawn.
First I fell when mounting - bad form.
Then on board I was able to stay,
But couldn't steer- the house got in the way.
Soon I was able to ride up the street.
I didn't know what I was about to meet.
By the side of the road tall weeds grew,
Hiding a trail toward which I flew.
At that place and time I met a horse.
My bike and I collided, of course.
Who was scared the most I cannot say,
Rider, horse, or me on that fateful day.
The horse kicked out as they're wont to do.
There's bad and good news I'll relate to you.
The broken spokes on the bike is the bad.
The good is the hoof just grazing this lad.
The rider was able to stay on his horse.
The outcome of this could've been much worse.
From this brief encounter what did I find?
"In life much is timing," sticks in my mind.

21. The Jackknife

The boy usually had a knife in his pocket.
This was a useful tool, so please don't knock it.
There was always something to cut, it seems,
Or maybe he whittled while dreaming his dreams.
He could carve a wooden dog, cat or horse.
Cut fingers were a regular result, of course.
Teachers hated knives for a simple reason.
Kids cut desk initials especially in spring season.
Two sets of initials surrounded with a heart.
When it identified the carver, it was not too smart.
The teachers had a point in being gruff,
Since the surface of the desk became quite rough.
The best place to carve initials was on a tree.
The beech was best you must agree,
Since the bark would heal and make a scar.
The initials would last in time quite far.
Many a man always carries his pocket knife,
Since it's a tool that's quite handy in life.
But not on airlines due to worldly strife.

22. Storm Drain

Walking down the street after it had rained,
We saw the way that it was drained.
The water ran through the grid to a pipe.
This was the large diameter concrete type.
We decided to trace where the big pipe went,
And found the small pond where the water was sent.
The pipe ended and was completely in view.
We found that it was big enough for us to crawl through.
We could not crawl on hands and knees,
Though we found the elbow crawl was a breeze.
This is the way that soldiers would crawl,
When they wanted to stay low and small.
We got to a catch basin up the street.
It had a vertical opening that was rather neat.
We could stand inside and look out and about.
When someone walked by, we'd give a shout.
This surprised a neighborhood kid or two.
Then we thought if someone told, we're in the stew.
So we decided to scoot back out
Being there was probably bad, no doubt.
Later we thought about getting stuck,
Or having a big rain storm we couldn't duck.
This would have been it, when we ran out of luck.

23. Brownie

We didn't have a dog for a while.
Boys should have one. Dogs make us smile.
A dog followed my cousin home one day.
His family just wouldn't let it stay.
My uncle asked if we'd like to have her.
There was no question for me, no sir.
We named her Brownie and brought her home.
We hoped she would no longer roam.
Dogs were as free as kids back then.
They could come and go as their wild kin.
One day Brownie just stayed away.
I called and whistled for the rest of the day.
She'll find her way is what my parents said.
The next day I went looking full of dread,
And I found her nearby tied up with a chain.
I knocked on the door having lost my pain.
"That's my dog," I said to the man at the door.
"My cousin gave her to me," I did implore.
But he replied in words I hated to hear.
"Blackie went missing. She was lost I fear.
"But now she's home where she's meant to be."
I was crushed which he saw when he looked at me.
There are truly good people in this crazy place.
This man was one when he saw my face.
"Take the dog. You'll give her a good home."
And so Brownie (or Blackie) no longer did roam.
But this, dear friend, is not the end of the tale,
For no matter our wants, we often will fail.
A little while later distemper she had.
There was no treatment or shots, it's sad.
And his tears didn't help this poor young lad.

24. Guinea Pig

I'm not sure where the guinea pig was from,
But I adopted her as my special chum.
When I came in the house, she knew it was me.
Pig made a high pitched squeak, it was glee.
Animal psychologists say animals have no emotions,
But those in the know, see love and devotion.
A lowly rodent can love her boy,
And show this love by expressing joy.
I took care of pig and fed her greens.
I gave her attention and kept her pen clean.
We went on the lawn for fresh grass and clover.
Pig wandered about but not all over.
But then one day something spooked her bad.
She ran in the ivy and bushes we had.
I called and I searched but without success.
My guinea pig was lost, oh what a mess.
We never found pig, my sister and me,
And all because of my naivete.
A little leash or a fence, you see,
And I'd be prepared for any eventuality.

25. The Kitten

Of all the pets that one can own,
The cutest are kittens and pups not grown.
We had several over the years.
One of them brought me mostly tears.
She was just the sweetest little thing.
When playing with her, my heart would sing.
My buddies and I were playing one day
On this slopping ground across the way.
From where we were I could look down,
And see the street, which brought a frown.
Our little kitten was standing there.
She should be safe. Did I have to care?
A truck was coming on the other side,
But the driver made a turn so wide,
He hit the kitten, squashed her flat.
Why did he do a thing like that?
I know he meant to do that deed,
And since, I've found that nasty breed
Think nothing much of hurting others, it's sad.
No matter what, they're just plain bad.
My hopes on this I shouldn't dwell
Just let them have a place in hell.

26. Cindy

Cindy the cat was our family pet.
She was the neatest cat I've ever met.
She came from Grandpa. My sister named her.
This was a mistake, but none will blame her.
Cindy's really a tomcat, forgive the mixup.
Grandpa, the farmer, had done a fix up.
Cindy's name stayed with "her," it's OK.
People always refer to cats as "her" anyway.
It took a while for Cindy to do it,
But she trained us well, we got through it.
If she wanted out, she scratched by the door.
We're fast to avoid shredding wallpaper more.
To enter the house, she scratched on the screens.
She soon taught us that's what she means.
Cindy was odd, I'll have to say.
She liked strange things. You'll say, "No way."
When Mom pealed potatoes at the kitchen sink,
Cindy jumped up, balanced on the brink,
And pawed at Mom's hand for a piece of peel.
For her, cucumber skin also had its appeal.
Cindy was quite an affectionate cat.
This is unusual, they're not like that.
When people came by for a brief visit,
The cat would jump on a lap to sit.
This was especially true if you didn't like cats.
Old Cindy seemed to have a sense about that.
One time a strange car was parked out front.
The old cat heard, our comments were blunt.
A short while later, and what should we see,
Our Cindy was backed against it taking a pee.
For a good many years she was our favorite pet,
But as with us all, old she did get.
In animal heaven, they'll like her, I bet.

27. Ant Fights

The boy always wanted to be in the know.
He watched the world both high and low.
Sometimes his interest was the busy ant.
From which he learned much, you'll grant.
The carpenter ants are big and black.
They'll get in your house through any crack
And destroy the place by weakening beams.
They have no redeeming value, it seems.
Another ant was about half as big.
These were red, and in the ground they'd dig.
The red ones were extremely fast.
You'd see them come and then they're past.
Across the curb, and jump to the street,
As insects go they're rather fleet.
He wondered if they were put together,
Would they get along or fight each other.
Would slow and strong win this race,
Or would speed take the winner's place.
To make it more even, two red and one black.
The reds were rather quick in their attack.
The reds bit first and held on tight,
But then were dispatched with a single bite.
What did he learn from this small test,
Fast is good but strength is best.
If fast ever wants to win the fight,
Then don't get caught, and you'll be all right.

28. Deer Flies

Mark Twain had a story about the fly.
He figured Noah made a special stop, and why?
He forgot the fly with animals two by two.
I damn sure would have left it, wouldn't you.
For the fly there must have been a plan,
To make all animals suffer, including man.
One type that sure gave us kids a fit
Was the deer (or three corner) fly, to wit.
Whenever we walked on paths in the wood,
They'd fly around our heads looking for blood.
They'd land on our hair and then flit away,
Just before we'd swat to our dismay.
We rarely were able to squash the things,
And occasionally we'd receive their stings.
Being inventive and not wanting to be bled,
We cut leafy branches to wave about our heads.
Then we discovered a strange thing if you will.
These flies couldn't find us if we stood still.
They had Doppler eyesight to get their kill.

29. Wild Honey

Dad and Uncle Art had found a special tree.
It had a hollow that was home to some bees.
We always watched for things like this.
Natures bounty was not to be missed.
They waited for a day that was cold enough,
So the bees would be nice instead of gruff.
They didn't use smoke like bee keepers do,
When they work with the hive and anger a few.
Bees aren't normally found in the wild.
They're domesticated immigrants who can be riled.
The men filled a pail with the wild honey.
It's free since the bees wouldn't take any money.
They left enough for the bees' survival,
And they'd be lively again with spring's arrival.
We kept the honey in the porch's cool.
Any bees still there would surely be fooled.
They wouldn't buzz around and try to sting us
When we had all this tastiness they did bring us.
I'd take a big bite of the comb of wax,
Chew it up. It made great snacks.
With one bite, I had a close squeak.
A bee had thawed and stung my cheek.
If I had swallowed that bee instead,
He'd have stung my throat, and I'd be dead.
A closed up throat will ruin your day.
So pay attention kids for what moms say,
And chew every bite thoroughly. That's the way.

30. Grandpa's Farm

Both my folks were raised on farms.
I guess for them it'd lost its charms.
My Dad left school at the end of grade eight.
From there business school was his fate.
For a profession Mom studied to be a nurse.
To this high level, she was the first.
Farming on a small scale is pretty tough.
Most, after the struggles, have had enough.
The farm was lost on my father's side
When the depression hit and his folks died.
But my other grandpa had held his own,
A small dairy farm with daughters grown.
We visited for a week each summer there.
This was a great adventure without compare.
I had more fun for which most would strive.
To help Grandpa I'd get up early at five.
First build a fire in the wood stove for Gran,
Then milk the cows and feed them their grain.
Pasteurize the milk before the truck takes it away.
They did more work before breakfast than most do in a day.
Breakfast was a farmer's true and tried,
With eggs, bacon, and potatoes all fried.
Toast dipped in bacon fat and pie
Provided the energy for them to get by.
Some days were spent bringing in hay,
To provide for the cows on the cold winter day.
Mucking out the barn gave them a yield,
Manure that was spread to fertilize the field.
Running a dairy farm meant work each day,
And the work was hard in every way.
Part of Sunday afternoon was for ease.
They'd sit on the porch for summer's breeze.
The animals needed caring for without cease.

The feeding and milking ended the peace.
Some think that farm folks are not well bred.
My Grandpa was cultured and also well read.
He educated three daughters when it rarely was done,
And worked at farming from sun to sun.

31. Work Horses

No tractor was used on Grandpa's farm.
A team of horses was his right arm.
They pulled all the things a tractor would,
The plow, the harrow, and loads of wood.
Grandpa had each of the machines he'd need
For raising the hay for his cows' feed.
All horse drawn machines had a driver seat,
Except the wagon where he stood on his feet.
Every few years he replanted the hay
When too many weeds got in the way.
He cut it several times a season
The number varied, rainfall the reason.
First he mowed, then after a day,
The machine was used that turned the hay.
Later it was raked into many a row,
Which at gathering time the horses would follow.
The team moved forward at a steady pace.
Uncle threw the hay. Grandpa put it in place.
The wagon was piled with a rather big load,
The hay hanging down almost touching the road.
Grandpa got the horses to stop and start,
Turn right, turn left, back up the cart.
I learned about horses, they're not like a pet.
They work pretty hard for the care that they get.
That's why grandpa warned me more than once.
Don't go in the stalls. Don't act like a dunce.
Of course, the warning was a sirens' call.
First the horse pushed me against the stall wall.
Then he stepped on my foot with iron shoe.
I got away from there pretty fast, wouldn't you?
Everyone examined my foot with wonder.
No broken bones resulted from my blunder-
The silver lining of the cloud I was under.

32. The Colt

The colt was born late in the fall.
He'd never been out of the barn at all.
He felt safe and warm by his mother's side.
All he needed she would provide.
The horses had it easy on a winter day.
Mostly they slept and ate oats and hay.
Mom was there and the barn was nice.
No worry about the winter snow and ice.
But spring arrived with its higher sun.
Time for the colt to venture out for fun.
Grandpa put on the halter to lead him out
The colt wouldn't move with pull or shout.
The mare was brought out with no more luck.
Then the hired man tried and slipped in the muck.
Finally, with two men pulling and two with a push,
They got the colt outside in a rush.
Why so much trouble with one so small?
He was still a baby, but that's not all.
This work horse baby was fifteen hands tall.

33. Losing The Cows

It's Sunday afternoon and we're sitting around.
Milking time approaches. The cows must be found.
They're in the far pasture grazing for the day.
"I can get them," I volunteered right away.
The cows know the time and will want to come in.
If they're not milked, there'll be a big din.
Their udders get so full, they'll be in pain.
They must return to the barn, that's plain.
Grandpa figures there's no problem here,
The cows know the way, nothing to fear.
I walk to the far pasture down the road.
The cows are waiting there as I was told.
They start walking when I open the gate.
Oh no, I forgot, I hope I'm not too late.
The road passes other fields back to the barn.
The closed gate there causes my alarm.
I start running to get there first.
The cows see this and put on a burst.
They're running right past the gate, oh no.
I get there and open it and through some go.
Finally, I get the remainder in tow
With a lot of racing both to and fro.
Did I learn anything from this event of dread?
Yes, there is no substitute for planning ahead.

34. Grandpa and Energy

Well before the modern meaning, Grandpa was green.
Then, this designation would cause him to vent his spleen.
He wasn't inexperienced nor was he naive.
He worked hard on his farm, you better believe.
His animals ate grass and hay plus some grain.
Their manure replenished the soil, the gain.
He only had to add lime now and then
To replace the calcium, and the soil to sweeten.
Horses pulled the machines, thus using no gas.
For the occasional drive to town, we'll give him a pass.
Each fall the horses pulled loads of wood.
Only straight grain was used, so splitting was good.
Grandpa's body was warmed twice in this way,
The furnaces heat and the wood splitting each day.
House and barn did have electric light,
But he minimized its use to only a mite.
We can't live like Grandpa whatever the need.
There isn't enough land for wood lot and feed,
And we can't raise our energy it must be agreed.

35. Grammar School

By modern standards our school was small.
There were only seven classrooms in all.
Including kindergarten, just one per grade.
With only twenty one kids in ours we had it made.
Seven teachers, a principal, and her aide,
Plus the custodian were the full brigade.
Not exactly a one room school house.
We had no complaints. We did not grouse.
For our egress there were three doors.
You only went through the one that's yours.
Boys never went in girls nor girls in boys,
And we only entered with the bell's loud noise.
Each classroom had a cloak room with hooks,
No lockers for your stuff and books.
Desks were like new ones but all of wood.
Each had an ink well, in the corner it stood.
A favorite trick of the boys back then
Was to dunk a girl's braid instead of a pen.
We had a break from our work each day
For cookies and milk. Two cents we'd pay.
The government subsidized this for reasons of health,
And didn't collect where there's lack of wealth.
We had recess outside to clear our heads.
When it rained, we tumbled indoors instead.
We had reading and writing and arithmetic.
Plus history and geography which did the trick.
No one was afraid to memorize by rote,
For math tables this certainly gets my vote.
Now kids are exposed to so much more,
And yet so many don't know the score.
One wonders what they go to school for.

36. School Trips

In grammar school the teachers were great,
And we the students, liked this trait.
Big risks, they were often willing to take
With a group of kids out on a "date."
The trips to New York we liked the best.
Our chaperones didn't seem so stressed.
We started by walking to the station, a mile.
There for the train we waited a while.
A train to Hoboken, then on the ferry,
Into the city, then it wasn't so scary.
We saw the tall buildings, the Empire State,
And stopped at the Automat where we ate.
The Statue of Liberty was a great stop.
We climbed inside right up to the top.
Enterprise, the carrier, was at the pier.
We had the full tour and saw all the gear.
The Museum of Natural History we liked best.
For keeping our interest, it passed the test.
The art museums we saw were OK, I guess,
Though not for pre-teens, I must confess.
There were no complaints each time we got home.
We'd gladly go back to the city to roam.
Being so impressed by trips into town,
I convinced my folks I'd travel on my own.
Now, parents would never, their kids not grown,
Let them travel that far on a train all alone.
With pedophiles and muggers perhaps they're right.
Maybe no one's safe in the big city day or night.
Also, teachers and mothers wouldn't take such a crew,
Since they'd be afraid that someone would sue.

37. The Tree

Each year our school had a large fir tree.
It was tall and full- the best there could be.
It was placed in the hall for all to see.
The teachers spent hours of their own time
Decorating their tree._It was in its prime,
The sight of which was truly sublime.
Every piece of tinsel was lined up just so.
It looked like icicles all in a row,
Not like tinsel we kids would throw.
This was a Christmas tree- no doubt.
It did no harm, but now it's out.
Thus, go our traditions, with nary a shout.

38. Ode to Mr. Coombs

Mr. Coombs was the janitor at our school.
He wielded more than a broom as his tool.
Watching the furnace was his biggest care.
He had to shovel coal by fires glare.
Things were not automatic in those days,
So physical work was required in many ways.
He cleaned all the classrooms and the halls,
Emptied the trash, and washed spots on the walls.
During the warm weather he mowed the lawn.
In winter he shoveled snow with muscled brawn.
He raised the flag and took it down
He worked quite hard with nary a frown.
If he had spare time, he'd fix a chair,
Or mop up messes both here and there.
There was one thing that was truly funny.
Mr. Coombs was disciplinarian for many.
If sitting in the corner or out in the hall,
Was a punishment that was too small,
The perp was sent to help Mr. Coombs
Down in the basement in the furnace rooms.
Of course, the teachers were never told,
This was a great adventure about to unfold.
The boys really loved to help this man,
And maybe some misbehaved as a plan.
Mr. Coombs was the only man we saw,
So you can understand his draw.
Of course, now my school would have two,
And other than cleaning, there's not much to do.
No one would dream of a kid working crew.

39. Team Sports

We had no real organized sports except at school.
No Little League, no Pop Warner, no games with rules.
The school teams were hard to plan is seems
With only seven in class to man the teams.
They dipped into the fifth grade to fill
The soccer and softball teams with less skill.
We played other grammar schools now and then
And always lost by scores far from even.
Interestingly, we played softball at our young age.
For older kids baseball was the rage.
Now kids play baseball, and the women
Are the softball players as well as the men.
We made our own rules for after school games.
Tackle basketball was one that was none too tame.
We wrestled some but most would skip.
They didn't want their knees to rip.
Their moms were tired of sewing the tear,
So they laid down the law to me and each peer.
"Be careful what you do with the clothes that you wear."

40. Kid Brother

My brother and I were eight years apart.
We didn't play together so much to start.
But now and then with him a bit older,
We'd play with trucks and maybe tin soldier.
Compared to twelve, he was still a tyke,
And for others to see us, that I didn't like.
One day we're playing out front in the dirt.
You wouldn't expect that this would hurt.
My Mom thought it was nice of me
To play with my brother where all could see.
But then embarrassment of the worst kind,
Worse than anything I'd had in mind.
Who should drive by right down the street,
But the last person I'd want to meet.
My sixth grade teacher waved at me,
And there I was for all to see.
But she didn't tell my class about it.
She didn't climb a mountain and shout it.
I survived this potential cause of pain,
And even for me there was some gain.
People don't notice and could care less.
It's all in your mind, as you should guess.
Who cares about embarrassing things you do.
Others surely don't and neither should you.

41. Clarinet

The teacher had said we'd have music lessons,
So having an instrument was the suggestion.
I told my folks that I should have one.
They thought this was good, so it was done.
I guess the rationale was my sister's piano.
They knew my reaction to those lessons was, "Oh, no."
They bought me a clarinet which was used,
A wise decision, since it might be abused.
I was good about practice, at least for a time.
It soon got tiresome, so I committed the crime.
I just didn't practice as much as I should.
The feeling I had was I'd never be good.
We had concerts with other grammar schools.
We all played so badly we felt like fools.
The clarinet can easily provide loud squeaks.
You should blow just right not puffing your cheeks.
Also, getting my fingers to move with speed,
I just couldn't do. I played badly all agreed.
When I went to junior high, it was time to quit.
I'm sorry folks, that I couldn't stay with it,
I think any instrument would give me a fit.

42. Halloween

Like now, Halloween was important for us.
We got ready for the day without much fuss.
Nobody bought a costume except some had a mask.
We created our getup, from what you may ask?
Old clothes and the rag bag often would do,
Especially for a hobo where nothing is new.
A few smudges applied to the face with black.
Completing the picture was a stick tied sack.
An old sheet was a popular drape.
Worn on the back, it made a good cape.
If you cut some holes, two at most,
You had a complete costume for being a ghost.
Cross dressing was often given tryouts.
I went once as a girl. I had my doubts.
Now one shouldn't take offense when none is meant,
But Mom said something. My psyche was bent.
"You'd make a good girl," she said to me.
Yuch! Nothing was worse as she should see.
Girls don't come with a build like mine.
This didn't matter, I took it as a sign.
Dress like a girl? I'd always decline.

43. The Old House

Up the street at the edge of town,
Was a decrepit old house that was falling down.
No one had lived there for many years,
And it was an attractive nuisance for me and my peers.
A root cellar opened at the side of a hill.
They'd stored apples there because of the chill.
We found that this was an unpleasant place
Due to the smell of mold in that damp space.
In the yard there was dug an uncovered well.
Kids were careful there and no one fell.
We didn't want anyone to come to harm.
There was no Lassie to sound the alarm.
We boys one day had heard some talk.
The girls that evening would take a walk,
To see if any of the stories were true.
Were there any ghosts in that old venue?
At once we decided to get there first
And provide a little surprise- the worst.
But somehow unbeknownst to the guys
A dad had heard about our planned surprise.
At the appointed time, we boys were in place.
Too bad in the dark, we could see no face.
Soon we heard the girls approaching the door.
This was the time we had waited for.
Then suddenly we heard something strange,
An eerie laugh and what sounded like chains.
The boys scooted right past the girls and out the door.
We'd heard enough and desired no more.
We all ran down the street a way,
With enough excitement for one day.
A little bit later, it was maybe a week,
We heard something that a dad did leak.
How the tricksters were tricked, so to speak.

44. Scouts

My friend next door had become a scout.
He told me that I should try it out.
They met at the church where I was a member.
Too bad that my birthday was not 'til December.
One had to be twelve to join the troop.
Our leader said I was OK for his group.
He could see that I really wanted to fit.
It was OK to stretch the rules a bit.
Two service men had each become a vet,
And wanted to help some kids they'd met.
Our troop was less formal than most would be.
We only had neckerchiefs and hats you see.
We learned the things that scouts should learn,
Oath, motto, law and to do a good turn.
There were camp outs, summer camp and hikes.
Things that an active kid really likes.
Camp craft is learning about the outdoors,
Building fires, cooking, pitching tents and more.
To learn to swim was my personal goal,
Which I did with determination and soul.
There are so many things not taught in school.
We learned great stuff that I found cool.
But everything ends with good reason or not.
This happened to us for some silly old rot.
We could meet there no more, the church people said,
Since only two scouts were members it was pled,
And so on good Christian values they tread.

45. War Effort

Way back we recycled, it was natural to do,
Since the value of things, we all knew.
But during the war, there's no question which,
Everyone collected stuff with hardly a bitch.
Milk, beer, and soda bottles were always turned in.
We collected all cans because of the tin.
Scrap steel, old rags, fat drippings and all,
Went for the war, no effort too small.
Quarters for savings stamps, we kids paid in,
Then for seventy five, a bond was the trade in.
We got it for eighteen seventy five- the deal.
After ten years it was worth twenty five for real.
We had junk men who often came to buy.
For scrap metal, the prices seemed pretty high.
On one of my wanderings through the wood,
I found an old car. It was rusted but good.
The engine, fenders and other parts were gone,
But the frame was still there all alone.
I gave it a heft. It was easy enough.
So end over end, though to home would be tough.
My friends I'm sure, must have thought I was nuts.
It was a challenge for me, no ifs, ands, or buts
Unlike Sisyphus, I prevailed with my labors at last.
And got the frame home, though not very fast.
I got a whole dollar as I knew I would,
But I proved to myself- I did what I thought I could.

46. Model Planes

Back in the days of World War Two,
We had much interest in all that flew.
We'd study the pictures of every airplane,
And could probably identify most of the same.
There were American and British and perhaps
Some of Russian and German and Japs.
 In retrospect I find it strange
That production of toys did not really change.
The government had the economy planned.
The war effort had spread throughout the land.
But model planes were available for us,
Keeping the home front happy I trust.
One type plane came in Wheaties or such,
As models go these just weren't so much.
They were made all of paper with a penny for weight.
They flew quite nicely, but landings weren't great.
If you were smart, you'd fly over grass.
We weren't, so they were destroyed en masse.
Now paper and balsa, they're easily made.
Cut out the parts with a razor blade.
Stick them together with airplane glue,
Which joins the parts sometimes to you.
Each plane was powered by an elastic band,
So they didn't fly very far over land.
We found by experience that landings were hard.
Our models didn't survive so well getting jarred.
I arrived at a solution to save them all.
I mounted my planes on my bedroom wall.
They stayed there awhile not being used.
Until I thought of a way to be amused.
I knew about planes that crashed in fire,
So I lit each one, the results were dire.
Out the window they flew and crashed in the yard.
Not all of the fun is in building, though hard.
Some fun can be found in results that are charred.

47. The Victory Garden

Our street had dormant farmland near.
There was a great place for gardens here.
To help the war effort was the goal.
Raising some veggies would be our role.
We'd tried a garden in our yard before,
But too much shade and the soil was poor.
Someone spread manure to help plants grow,
And a tractor plowed and harrowed just so.
The land was divided into many a plot.
To work hard here was now our lot.
We planted seed in measured row.
The right depth and spacing we should know.
Dad knew about such things from years past,
When his dad had taught him, and lessons last.
We pulled the weeds and hoed around.
This cut evaporation and rain could soak the ground.
The only insecticide we had for the garden bug,
Was nicotine based. It was more of a drug.
So we, usually me, picked bugs by hand,
And squished them between fingers. It wasn't so grand.
As the summer warmth made them thrive,
Veggies of our labors started to arrive.
We ate our fill of things in season.
Tomatoes and corn are best with reason.
Sun warmed tomatoes right off the vine,
As close as one gets to the Devine.
Fresh picked corn dropped in pot aboil
Tastes like heaven. It's worth the toil.
There always was more than we could eat,
Mom would can the rest for a winter treat.
There were no home freezers then
For saving until the winter season when
We wanted a taste of the good earth's gift,
To give the winter taste buds a lift.
So few people bother with gardens now.
They miss communing with the earth somehow.

48. War Maps

During the war the papers always had a map
Showing where action was for this at home chap.
Early on people said, "Guadalcanal, where's that?"
The map gave an answer from where I sat.
Go northeast a bit from east Australia.
The map gave directions that wouldn't fail ya.
Each of the Pacific islands was given a name
Where Marines and Army got their fame.
Tarawa, Iwo Jima, and also Saipan,
All part of the generals' plan.
Of the European theater, we were all aware.
We knew Italy and France and the Nazis' lair.
But when our troops went ashore on D-Day,
Nobody seemed to know where Normandy lay.
We kids found it on a map at school.
About the war we always were cool.
I guess geography came naturally to me.
All the world was there for us to see.
It saddens me now, that kids don't know
Much about anywhere they'd care to go.
What use is geography you may say.
It's just to be educated, this is part of the way.
When you don't know "wheres", it causes dismay.

49. Rationing

Some things were scarce for us in the war.
Rationing was tried to even the score.
People got stamp filled ration books for trade,
These were used for each purchase made.
The scarcer food stuffs were sugar, butter and meat.
Oleo the butter substitute was rather neat.
We mixed in the color, it was white like lard.
To make it the yellow of butter was hard.
I was with my dad up town one day,
When a strange man ran up with a bray.
"They've got butter at the A and P," He'd yell,
And repeated over and over like a pealing bell.
He was excited like he'd struck gold ore.
Some people by scarcity are affected more.
Tooth paste wasn't rationed, but you had to trade
The old empty tube, since of tin it was made.
Tin and rubber were imported from afar,
And the supply of these was stopped by the war.
Gasoline was rationed. Some filled their need,
If their job was important, then it was agreed,
That they'd get enough for their daily ride.
It was a criminal offense if they lied.
My Dad put the car on blocks off the floor,
And he walked the three extra miles or more.
This added to the distance walked on the route.
By the end of the day, he was really worn out.
Compared to other nations involved in the war,
We had no real complaints on this score.
Would people get by now? I think they'd need more.

50. Building Toys

I liked to build various things as a boy.
We had the construction type of toy.
Blocks were popular, but these I'd outgrown.
Little kids use them, but I still had my own.
You could add them to the Lincoln log set
To broaden the assortment of buildings you'd get.
Combining these with erector set and railroad track
Would result in a city if you had the knack.
I never had soldiers to add to my play,
And tinker toys were new in that day.
There was certainly enough stuff with my imagination
To construct whatever I wanted with variation.
Now it saddens me that kids don't build,
It seems their creative instincts are chilled.
Follow the directions for assembling a toy.
Don't vary from this. There's no inventive joy.
Could they make their own Godzilla or Tron.
Scramble up all those pieces and have some fun.

51. Radio Programs

Back at the dawn of the modern age,
Radio programs were all the rage.
About old time radio, you may have no clues,
Since now it's music, talk, traffic, and news.
There were radio programs back in the day
Like TV with no pictures, you could say.
Most families had one by the living room wall,
Which was listened to by one and all.
Mom and Dad got the soft easy chairs.
The kids lay on the floor. We had no airs.
Some people made sure they always heard
Their favorite shows. They missed no word.
Old shows could be put on every day
Actors read their scripts, the easy way.
The only extra was the sound effects man.
The hardest job went to the writing clan.
Since they had to have scripts ready on time.
No excuses accepted by reason or rhyme.
Not being able to see required imagination.
Words and sound effects gave inspiration.
I didn't feel the need to listen each day
To the Lone Ranger or Superman's, "Up, up, and away."
Most shows in the afternoon were a quarter hour.,
And to some kids, they had their power.
Some moms listened to the daily soaps.
We had no interest. They seemed like dopes.
Evening and Saturday shows were a half hour long.
Listening to these you couldn't go wrong.
Duffy's Tavern where the elite meet to eat.
Fibber McGee's closet just couldn't be beat.
Amos and Andy was popular as any.
"Did you listen?" was asked by many.
Now there's so much for us to choose from,
Nobody talks about the shows with a chum.
Maybe we don't want people to think that we're dumb.

52. Movies

The walk to the movies was a four mile round trip.
This was not so much, we could do a good clip.
Movies were pretty popular during the war.
People had money to spend with the promise of more.
Since only weekend afternoons were available to us,
Going was a treat with many a plus.
Now we get a feature film plus each coming attraction.
Then we had more for our satisfaction.
We had two features, except one if it was long,
Plus "Selected short subjects." How could we go wrong.
These always included a newsreel, usually about the war,
A cartoon with Bugs Bunny, Elmer Fudd and more.
One popular short was the lone Ranger.
Each episode ended with the hero in danger.
Here we were exposed to the Stooges Three.
Larry, Moe, and Curly were the best combo for me.
The brothers Marx, fat Ollie and Stan,
Bud and Lou were shorts that they ran.
They had one regular item we could do without.
A women's style report made us boo and shout.
The bargain for us was the cost of two bits.
An hour's wage for ten year olds, this fits.

53. The Greenhouse

The greenhouse was located just up the road,
Misplaced amongst houses and our abode.
Mr. Garlic (no kidding) ran it with wife.
He also worked full time- a busy life.
My Dad helped out there now and then.
They were co-workers, you see, both mailmen.
To watch the work, I went with my Dad.,
And saw what they did, a curious lad.
I asked if I could have a job too.
It was summer with not a whole lot to do.
My Mom thought this was a bit much for me,
But my Dad was wise and said, "Let's see."
"If he thinks he can, then he can."
I had no doubts, I could be a man.
In retrospect it was quite a lot.
One doesn't realize, a greenhouse is hot.
I worked all day the whole summer long,
Twenty five cents an hour. Was this so wrong?
I watered carnations and pulled the weeds.
I replanted cactus and ivy and filled other needs.
Plants were started in sand so wet,
Cut off pieces new roots would get.
Each piece was planted in a small pot,
And to the five and dime we sold a lot.
I'll always remember the cactus thorn,
The punctures that did my thumbs adorn,
But that's what the job required of me,
And if nothing more I learned, you see,
That I'd never pick as my life's work,
A greenhouse job. For taking one I'd be a jerk.
On the light side and in summation,
My favorite flower has always been the carnation.

54. Depression Lessons

Life was never easy about the time of my birth.
People learned the hard way all about worth.
I was too young to remember those days.
My folks, however, just followed the ways
That helped them survive with enough to get by,
And we kids were taught the how and the why.
We were fortunate that our Mom and Dad
Had faith that things wouldn't always be bad.
Our parents were married just before the big crash.
My sister and I were born when there wasn't much cash.
As young ones we didn't know we were poor.
Frugality came naturally, that's for sure.
So I'll repeat the lessons that we learned.
In our minds they'll always be burned.
Turn out the light and close the door.
What do you think that money is for?
Do you want to heat the whole outdoors,
And light up like a mansion with seven floors.
Don't waste food, clean up your plates,
Think of the kids in very poor straights.
You're more healthy if raised in the cold.
"Keep the thermostat low," We always were told.
No heat upstairs except for the bath.
A curtain pulled closed stopped the heat's path.
With whatever you use, make do.
Make it last, it's up to you.
Monday is wash day, Tuesday's for repair.
Keep darning those socks to counter the wear.
Wear hand-me-downs, they're just like new.
Don't be too proud, it's not like you.
Buy food in bulk, it's cheaper that way.
Can veggies and fruit for a later day.
In all these examples the lesson is clear.
You're not just being cheap as it appears.
You're saving the earth's bounty for future years.

55. Earning Money

I got an allowance when I was a kid.
That was what the modern parents did.
It wasn't so much even by standards of old,
But there was something I always was told.
Your money is very important to save.
The road to college this will pave.
You're good at school, especially in math.
Take engineering for a career path.
So working is what I wanted to do.
Of all the kinds, I did more than a few.
Rake that yard and mow that lawn,
Pull the weeds, these I had to be shown.
More than one flower was pulled by mistake.
Some I replanted with the hope they'd retake.
On occasion we had a snow day at school.
I'd earn extra money, a snow shovel my tool.
I worked a bit in the greenhouse as well.
For a steady income this surely was swell.
I babysat for kid and pet.
Though I'd say a pre-teen is not a good bet.
Parents were happy enough with my work,
But eating all the brownies made me a jerk.
Once I took care of a flock of hens.
Feed them and water them and get eggs from the pens.
Once the lady said to leave the eggs there.
We'll get chicks if the sitting hens take care.
Somehow she didn't know a rooster was needed.
A young boy's remarks just weren't heeded.
I learned from each job as I've said before.
Those things I'd rather do no more.
When grown up, I'll know the score.

56. Knickers

My family as you may be aware,
Only spent money with the greatest of care.
Hand-me-downs were the usual fare
With one older cousin I felt I had luck,
Cause some of the clothes really did suck.
One day the trend I tried to buck.
"Wear these knickers to school," my Mom had said.
I replied to her, "I'd rather be dead."
So I wore some old shorts to school instead.
Trouble was it was snowing that day.
I froze, but I made my point, I'd say.
No more outdated knickers, no way.

57. Gourmet Delights

Eating was a great adventure for us.
We didn't fool around or make a big fuss.
We tried things that might make you blanch.
We gave each idea a reasonable chance.
My sister and I liked an invention we made,
Some butter on bread with sugar overlaid.
I found that peanut butter always was great,
But it stuck to the roof of my mouth when I ate.
For my sandwich two additions I did embellish.
Mayonnaise worked well and so did pepper relish.
I always liked chocolate especially the dark,
But it wasn't always around to give me that spark.
My Mom had baker's chocolate, the unsweetened kind.
It was really quite bitter, but I didn't mind.
Take a spoonful of sugar with each small block,
And chew the mix carefully to avoid any shock.
If the mix was still bitter, then add more sweet.
It wasn't a Hershey bar but still was a treat.
I learned to make cookies at an early age.
When the folks went out, and there was nothing to pillage.
I got out the fixings and started from scratch.
I mixed the right portions for a small batch.
This wasn't a secret. My Mom could tell.
Though there was no evidence left except for the smell.
I even cleaned up the mess I had made.
Which is a pretty good idea after a larder raid.
You don't want Mom to ban such an escapade.

58. Haircuts

Without good reason one should never spend money.
Spending a quarter for a haircut? Don't be funny.
Mom cut mine with scissors and comb.
She didn't use a bowl to cover my dome,
So when finished, I didn't look like Moe.
Never-the-less, I wouldn't mind spending the dough.
Other kids would always notice the cut,
And poke fun. They wouldn't keep their mouths shut.
Besides, I hated that itchy haircut feel
Of short cut hairs. For me it was a big deal.
When I earned some money, and it was mine to keep,
I went to the barber. I wasn't too cheap.
Of course, when I had kids of my own,
I cut their hair 'til they were full grown.
And guess who cut mine for many a year.
My loving wife and no one did jeer.
Possibly cause she does a great job, the dear.

59. Fishing

It was a bit of a hike to the fishing place.
We didn't mind. We walked a good pace.
Bridal paths ran back through the wood.
Crisscrossing everywhere so walking was good.
A stable's manure pile provided our bait.
The energetic worms sealed the fish's fate.
The fishing hole was narrow but long,
A good place to fish, you couldn't go wrong.
This lake was created by damning a stream,
And was dredged for depth it seems.
Any pole would do, except mine was real.
It didn't work so well though- no big deal.
The pole handle of cork was for extra hooks,
In case of snags on crannies and nooks.
No one needed much- no fancy stuff.
Jackknife, worm can, and stringer were enough.
We caught sun fish, crappies, perch, and cat.
All were pan fish, no bass and like that.
I once caught a pickerel with no bait on the hook.
This was one exciting thing in my book.
Each pan fish did put up a good fight.
This was enough for this kid, all right.
I always took my catch home for a meal.
No one would bother now, I feel.
My Mom cleaned the fish. She was raised that way,
I found out later what she didn't say.
Mom did this work with some dismay.

60. Black Walnuts

Out by the orchard, two black walnut trees grew.
No one seemed to want the nuts in my view.
One tree, the mother was a hundred feet tall.
The other, the daughter, was relatively small.
The nuts fall from the tree when still green.
They're not ripe yet thought they're smooth and clean.
I collected them in a cloth sack
Which I carried home thrown over my back.
Before use, they have to dry out and age.
The outside rind turning black is the gage.
I placed them out back to dry in the sun.
They should ripen nicely until they are done.
One day while walking home from school,
I thought, "Why I must be a fool."
What made me come to this conclusion
Was seeing a squirrel without confusion
Carrying a nut across the street
Preparing its larder for a winter treat.
I quickly moved the nuts to the cellar.
They'd dry just as well, safe from that feller.
When people think walnut, it's the soft English kind.
The black walnuts are the hardest nut you'll ever find.
When the maxim was coined, "A tough nut to crack."
They had in mind the walnut that's black.
Since no nut cracker can touch these nuts,
It's hammer on concrete, no ifs, ands, or buts.
Since we had to work so hard to eat,
The nuts made a rather special treat.
Those not eaten by us kids we'd take,
And add to the batter for muffin or cake.
This was a pleasant memory of my youth,
But I was disturbed by an unpleasant truth.
Years later I walked where the great tree stood.
The valuable walnut tree had been cut for wood.

61. Berries

One activity fit for man and child
Was picking nature's gifts grown wild.
Where woods, old orchards, and fields abound,
One can find out where the fruits are found.
Blackberries were most abundant I felt.
Take a big bucket and one for your belt.
Wear long pants. I never wore short,
And a long sleeve shirt to avoid the hurt.
These berry bushes are loaded with thorn
Whose scratches your arms would soon adorn.
The technique I found to work one day,
Pick the closest bush then push it away.
Use your foot and press to ground.
Don't worry, the vine will soon rebound.
Leave the big bucket where it will be found.
Fill the small one and empty before full round.
Once when picking I found a robin's nest
Amongst the berries, vines, and the rest.
The babies thought that I was dad.
They opened wide for any worms I had.
I left that spot as soon as I could.
Parent birds attack, and I knew they would.
I got my big pail and called it a day.
In a couple weeks the birds would be on their way.

62. Berry Uses

When we picked berries we ate our fill.
I remember Mom's pies and muffins still.
She made jellies and jams, but no juice.
Blackberries and blueberries were canned for winter use.
On a few occasions Dad tried making wine,
Though he never drank any. We didn't dine.
He'd been successful making saki of course.
That's Japanese wine with the kick of a horse.
When Dad tested his wine with a bit of dread,
He found blackberry and elderberry vinegar instead.
We used some, but most was stored,
Until years later when I mentioned the hoard
To my friend's dad who liked vinegar made from fruit.
He'd use it on salads and for cooking to boot.
So our labors in picking and processing the berry
Had worthwhile uses, but all culinary.
If we want some wine for a fancy meal,
We'll buy it and get better taste I feel.

63. Hunting

My Dad and I went hunting in my youth
These were more like woods walks, to tell the truth.
The unlucky squirrel or rabbit was our game.
There were never birds or deer for us to claim.
These rodents were smart, I kid you not.
Squirrels knew they could avoid being shot.
They'd stay on the opposite side of the tree,
Away from the guy with the gun you see.
My Dad was the one to shoot the gun.
A double barrel shotgun's too much for the young.
We took our catch home for a meal.
Fried squirrel or rabbit, we'd eat with zeal.
Some people would be put off by the thought of this.
Eating an animal you'd shot, they'd gladly miss.
In general, modern folks from nature are divorced.
Preparing an animal to eat- only if forced.
We as a race have hunted for a countless age.
For those who still do, some may take umbrage.
If we don't take care, we'll return to that page.

64. In Retrospect

This grandpa had a great youth as I've said.
I did wild things. I didn't wind up dead.
Though some escapades were a bit much,
I got a few scratches, and bruises and such.
I suffered some frostbite from my winter play
When my toes get cold, I'm aware to this day.
I waited for football for my first bone break,
When I caught my pinky, for goodness sake.
My first stitch was during a root canal,
When I was nineteen (an elbow from a pal).
My finger's still crooked, my tooth is still there.
I wish I could say the same for my hair.
My luck was determined by time and space.
You may be as lucky or fall on your face
We can hope you'll have memories sweet.
About adventures you've had that were so neat..
However, I think kids are protected too much.
They miss the fun and adventure and such.
Too many aren't close to animals and dirt.
Their immune systems never have to exert.
And having animals you can give love and get it,
And sometimes stuff happens. You have to let it.
You'll be hurt in life, there is no doubt
You will learn from this, you can make out.
Finally, kids don't exercise enough in organized play.
It can't take the place of walking each day.

Some remembrances are about life in the past.
It was how we survived. We made everything last.
In all ways I've been a frugal man.
I conserve money and things as much as I can
And now I find my life style is green.
All modern folks should know what I mean.

When you spend so much on stuff you don't need.
You're helping the environment decay with speed.

I repeat what I said in the title before.
My huckleberry days were, and are no more.
Now at the risk of being a bore,
Live directly. This is my messages' core.

Huckleberry Days Prequel

Contents

1. The Mean Cat

We shared our house with people next store.
They had a black cat I learned to abhor.
I remember nothing about the people there.
I sure remember that cat because of the scare.
The evil cat was given a name by Mom.
She decided to call it that Mean Old Tom.
The cat would stay by the door outside,
Run out and bite my ankle when I took my first stride.
With this aggressive action, he never broke the skin.
However, he did make me want to stay in.
For a time I thought if I had a dog pet,
He'd chase that darn cat whenever they met.
Dad had a good idea. Put a broom by the door,
And sweep the old tom. This would even the score.
The idea worked, and I had trouble no more.

2. Brownie the First

I was a youngster maybe about four.
We moved when I was five. This was before.
My Mom called her the Old Mother Dog.
She had a litter of pups. They had me agog.
Little Brownie I chose to be my pup.
I had to wait before I could pick him up.
They stayed in a box my Dad had made.
An old blanket on the bottom was laid.
This made a warm place for our dog pen.
They could stay close to their mom like in a den.
She nursed them, that's how they'd feed.
The mother dog provided for every need.
She washed the pups by lapping them.
For kids the bathtub was a better system.
The puppies didn't get hurt climbing over each other.
Sometimes they fell off when attached to their mother.
They stayed in the box until they could climb out.
Then in the kitchen they could scamper about.
Finally, after some begging I was told,
That my pup I could pick up and hold.
He climbed up my chest maybe looking for food.
Did he think I was mom taking care of the brood?
Brownie climbed up and gave me a lap.
A kiss from my puppy. I was one happy chap.
Then my folks announced one day,
The puppies were big enough to give away.
Couldn't we keep Brownie, I pled quite loud.
Only one dog per family was allowed.
I saw Brownie when he was full grown.
He didn't remember me. I thought he was my own.
I vowed that when I was big one day,
I'd have my own dog and never give him away.

3. Where Did God Stand?

Early on we're taught in Sunday school
About the bible, the commandments, the golden rule.
The Genesis story made a big hit with me,
How God created the heavens, the earth, and the sea.
He created all living things from heaven
And rested from this on day seven.
Probably many kids have thought the same
When contemplating the biblical claim.
This was what bothered me about Genesis.
Where did God stand while doing all this?

4. The Igloo

We had a pretty big snow one day.
Then the sun came out melting some away.
It's always nice when the sun is warm.
It keeps snow covered branches from harm.
Also, the snow is just right for making stuff,
But of snowmen and forts we'd had enough.
Dad said we should try making something new,
So we decided on building our own igloo.
The Eskimos make homes with blocks of snow.
Their snow packs hard when the cold winds blow.
We made ours by shoveling a big pile,
Then hollowing out the inside. It took awhile.
You can play with what you've made. It's fun.
But then after a while you find you're done.
So we thought of something truly spectacular.
We decided to smash it with the family car.
This was the best part of the project by far.

5. The Skunk

"What's that smell," we asked our Dad
"Why it smells like skunk." It was pretty bad.
Dad went to investigate and found the source.
A skunk had wandered into the basement, of course.
Here's a quandary. What should we do?
Don't upset the skunk or the effect you'll rue.
Dad left the bulkhead door open a bit.
The skunk didn't take our hint to spit.
Uncle Art was visiting, and they made a plan.
We kids were excluded. Was it a job for Superman?
My sister and I sat on the kitchen floor
Waiting for the smell to come through the door.
We held our noses in preparation
In case the men in their desperation
Had caused the skunk to let go a stream.
Then the house would smell worse then we could dream.
It seems the skunk decided not to stay,
And taking its time it walked away.
He'd added enough excitement to our day.

6. Kindergarten

I started kindergarten at four years of age.
It was Roosevelt school. Presidents' names were the rage.
The walk to school was a bit much for a little tyke,
But my Mom came along for the school going hike.
Then she'd meet me at the end of half a day.
It was normal to walk the youngest this way.
Older kids walked to and fro with each other.
There was no need to include a mother.
Nowhere in town was there a school bus,
But this was never a problem for us.
Kids learned to take care crossing the street
With less traffic, few cars would we meet.
Buses, of course, cut down on the danger
From cars and encounters with a stranger.
Now parents are overdoing safety a bit
When they drive to the bus and wait for it.

7. The New House

My Mom always wanted to own a house.
It took a lot to convince her spouse.
They managed to buy an odd shaped piece of land.
It was small but had room for a house to stand.
Unlike the procedures followed now,
They hired an architect to design what they'd allow.
The house was rather odd but truly unique,
And it was certainly better than renting by the week.
On Saturdays we'd go and watch the progress.
Dad did a few things to help the process.
My sister and I played around the yard.
I liked to watch. The work looked hard.
I watched the men unloading iron pipe.
Dad was really mad and started to gripe.
"I told you not to go near the truck."
This one time I was out of luck.
I replied, "You said don't go in front
"And I was in back. " I was rather blunt.
This was the only time in my youth
That Dad gave me a spanking to tell the truth.
He wanted to emphasize his point to me.
Since I had courted danger, you see.

8. Walking Home

We all went out to our new place.
Construction preceded at a steady pace.
My sister and I always found things to do.
We didn't pay attention. Dad gave us the cue.
"It's time to go," He called to us.
We weren't in a hurry like in catching a bus.
We dawdled and didn't get to the car.
Then suddenly realized when we got a jar.
Mom and Dad just weren't in view.
They had left us here as they'd threatened to do.
So we decided to walk back to our home.
We knew we could make it, the brave twosome.
My sister was seven, and I was five.
There were no doubts. We would strive.
We turned the corner, and what did we see?
The car was there where we hoped it would be.
Our parents had provided a lesson for us.
Please come when called without any fuss.
You should be thoughtful and courteous.

9. Incredible Journey

We moved to our new house in the late summer.
Everything was nice except for a bummer.
One point I've made concerning our ways.
Kids and animals were more free in those days.
We let our cat out as was usually done.
She didn't come back. Where had she run.
We whistled and called all the next day.
Mom had an idea of where she might stay.
We drove back to the old house, about two miles,
And found something that brought us smiles.
Back at her home was our old cat.
She knew how to get there and quickly, at that.
We picked her up and returned to our place,
But then she was gone again, leaving no trace.
We found her next day but left her there.
Maybe cats from old times, stay by their lair.
That was her home. Nothing new could compare.
As an adult I realized how our cat thought.
We had deserted her. What had we wrought?
Her hopes of our return had come to naught.

10. The Errant Couch

Our new house had a path not unlike a track.
Kitchen to hall, to living room, to dining room, and back.
This came in handy if I made Mom mad.
She would chase me when I'd acted bad.
The path was a raceway where I found
It was easy to evade her going around.
I had another activity that was a ball.
I'd run from the kitchen and down the hall,
Then dive over the end table and land on the divan,
Arriving just right on the cushions was the plan.
You know how young boys can be unaware.
I didn't notice the furniture was moved here to there.
That evening I ran. It was quite dark.
I dived at the right place, and then got a shock.
I landed flat on the floor. What a surprise.
There were no broken bones nor any black eyes.
I thought of a saying that night before sleep.
I now knew the meaning of look before you leap.

11. My Bedroom

As I said before, our house was truly unique.
This was apparent with my bedroom of which I must speak.
A walk-in-closet would describe it best.
By having my own room though, I felt I was blest.
It was L-shaped and was maybe five feet wide.
My built-in bed took all of one side.
There was a small closet and a shelf,
That could be a desk if I were an elf.
I didn't mind the small size of my room.
At least it was mine, but I shouldn't assume.
I was almost eight when my brother was born,
And a little while later, we needed a shoe horn.
Because then Bill came to share my space.
My bed went out. A bunk bed took its place.
Which wasn't really that big a deal.
I didn't spend much time there I must reveal.
Mostly, I did my homework on the dining room table,
The time honored place that's irreplaceable.
Our family were all big readers, it's true.
We shared the living room as considerate families do.
Thinking back, we both used our bedroom for sleep.
We didn't need privacy with no secrets to keep.

12. Walks with Dad

I really enjoyed my walks with Dad.
These were through the woods and fields we had.
I later realized these were familiar from his day,
Since he was raised but a half mile away.
He taught me about all the things we'd see.
How to identify each bush, bird, flower and tree.
Which berries were good, and which were not.
Which leaves had a good taste. There were not a lot.
Where were the springs if you wanted a drink.
Which berries to use for home made ink.
You could say he provided survival lore.
If I ever were lost, I'd know the score.
Sometimes I thought it was rather unfair
For me to ask if we could take the air.
My Dad walked each day on his mail route.
Walking with me was a mailman's holiday no doubt.

13. Transition

When I started first grade, I was only five.
A bit young for sure, and I might not thrive.
There were five boys with birthdays in the fall.
Parents were asked about enrolling us all
In a special program they'd planned for us.
A transition class that turned into a big plus.
We'd spend the morning each day in first grade.
Then for the afternoon, we had it made.
We had the kindergarten room to ourselves
With the pick of the toys that covered the shelves.
I don't remember the teacher a bit,
And of anything she taught us, not a whit.
What I do remember, it sticks in my mind,
The giant blocks that we kids did find,
Could be used to construct a walk in hut
With a window and a door that shut.
I have a feeling that giant wood blocks
Had a limited life span. They were as heavy as rocks.
They could collapse and hurt a young one,
And in that grade, it's not too much fun.
Now they have plastic for houses that are small,
But adults construct them. They're no fun at all.
Was our year in transition worthwhile on the whole?
Well, three of five made high school high honor role.

14. Bare Feet

School is out, we're free to run.
We're outside the house enjoying the sun.
The first thing to do is take off those shoes.
We can toughen our feet. It's what we choose.
Your feet are in shape for a full day's travel,
When you can run on driveway gravel.
Kids can do this better than the full grown.
Light weight means less pressure on a sharp stone.
However, on occasion our good times would fail,
When we didn't watch out and stepped on a nail.
Also, there was the painful time of woe,
When you didn't lift your feet and stubbed a toe.
You won't forget bending a toenail back.
It will grow back in time after such an attack.
After enough of these accidents plus some age.
Black high side sneakers became the rage.
The full uniform for us in the summer heat
Was dungarees with no shirt or socks on our feet.
After a while the sneakers smelled rather bad.
The dungarees got ragged which was not a fad.
Moms kept busy sewing patches on knees.
Soon the patches had patches to keep out the breeze.
We had our share of bruises and scratches,
But not like bare legged girls who had batches.
These wounds were okay with us blokes
Now pediatricians agree with our folks.
These are signs that indicate kids are active.
Better for health than being a TV captive.

15. Fighting Back

"Eddie's picking on me," I complained to Mom.
I was looking for some motherly balm.
This wasn't the first time I'd had this say,
About my next door neighbor's mean way.
After a few, "Poor dears," and such
And giving me the motherly touch,
Mom gave me some advice I needed,
And that this advice should be heeded.
She said,"You should stand up to an attack.
"If Eddie hits you, then hit him back."
So the very next time that Ed hit me,
I got incensed and swung one, two, three.
I managed to get him right in the nose,
And in that instant it had the color of a rose.
So Ed ran home bleeding all around.
I felt pretty good having stood my ground.
Ed's old grandmother banged on the door.
Complaining how I'd hit Ed. She'd stand no more.
She was forgetting that Ed was two years older.
"He should be able to hold his own," Mom told her.
It turned out from that day's end,
That Ed became my pretty good friend.

16. Wash Day

With a modern washer, turn it on and add soap.
Fill it with clothes. It can be done by a dope.
Come back in a while and fill the drier.
If I said this was a tough job, I'd be a liar.
Now in the good old days washing was a chore.
It took a full half day and maybe more.
When we built our house, Mom insisted that
In the cellar there would be two big sinks like vats.
To do the operation, you had to be skilled.
With soapy water the machine was filled.
The clothes were divided into several piles.
Then each was agitated for a while.
Next you'd feed each piece through the wringer,
And watch that you didn't catch a finger.
Wash in the washer, then soak in sink one.
Then on to the second, you've hardly begun.
Maybe six loads from white to dark with grime.
Each washed, soaked twice, and wrung three times.
You used the same water again and again.
The clothes came out quite clean even then.
Then the clothes were hung on the line to dry.
If Mom was lucky, she'd have a clear sky.
Later take the clothes off the line.
Sun dried clothes smelled really fine.
Then various items were set aside for repair.
Broken buttons replaced, socks darned by the pair.
The ironing was done on the following day.
Taking care of the clothes was a job with no pay.
However, it was better than the wash board any day.

17. Hang on Tight

Mom was doing the laundry in the cellar.
I was watching my brother, a cute little feller.
I couldn't comfort him when he started to fuss.
I carried him down. I wasn't nervous.
Our basement stairs ended facing a wall.
This was definitely not a place to fall.
Yet on the third step from the bottom, I tripped,
And aimed toward the wall with my head dipped.
I held my brother safe in my arms
While plowing head first, no thought of the harm.
It's strange how we instinctively protect the young
When it's natural to fall with arms out flung.
The baby was not hurt in any way
Nor strangely enough, neither was I that day.
The reason's my hard head kept injury at bay.

18. Walking Girls Home

For a brief period around grade two
A boy may feel there's something he can do.
He can walk a girl home from school,
And not feel that he's a perfect fool.
He's not concerned about the guys,
Who'll give him grief-a wimp in their eyes.
For a while I was that young lad.
I walked two girls, and felt quite glad.
I guess I was attracted to Lillian and Pat.
At the time they were friends, something like that.
Walking them home was out of my way,
But what's a little distance in that day.
We talked. About what, I haven't a clue.
It was exciting though, spending time with those two.
But then there arose that prohibition
That caused in me the inhibition.
Boys and girls are supposed to stay apart.
This has nothing to do with the heart.
At times we can both play in a group game,
But don't give the impression you like a dame.
That shouldn't happen 'til you're much older.
Then towards girls, you can act bolder.
In the meantime just do your duties,
And act as if the girls all have cooties.

19. Shoplifting

I think that kids can often be bad
Without even thinking, maybe following a fad.
When I was young, I got in trouble this way.
I followed what a friend did say.
It seems there was this store uptown.
Amongst the kids, it had renown.
The candy counter was right next to the door.
You could pick up a candy bar, maybe more,
And scoot right out, the merchandise not bought.
Then run down the street without being caught.
I had to try this, though I knew it was dumb.
I stood and examined the candy and gum.
I picked what I wanted and scooted out.
There was no commotion, no warning shout.
I had gotten my prize, and I was free,
But I learned that there was no glee.
Yes, I'd avoided being caught and its pain.
There was no embarrassment nor any strain.
I found for me, the lesson that was sent,
That the crime committed was the punishment.
Even when caught, many need no more.
"My God, what have I done," really evens the score.

20. Train Set

We couldn't wait for Christmas to arrive.
So on those mornings we got up at five.
At the same time our parents were tired,
Having stayed up late before they retired.
But we didn't notice and charged the tree
Expecting the best with childlike glee.
My favorite present was an electric train set.
Could there be anything better to get.
The train became a Christmas tradition,
Placed around the tree as an ornament addition.
In that sense it was a present for all,
But I got to play with it and have a ball.
My train was the standard Lionel brand.
It may have been ordinary, I thought it was grand.
Trains are neat, but their real worth should be,
In the making of buildings, roads, bushes and trees.
I had no permanent setup due to lack of space.
I never got involved in a special railroad place.
That's all right since I had a lot to do
Playing with models was less fun as I grew.

21. Getting a Piano

Her folks had an organ when Mom was young.
The idea of a piano from this had sprung.
My folks made inquiries and a free one was found.
It was an upright, player piano (with rolls) still sound.
This was pretty good for a boy like me,
Who from lessons, just wanted to stay free.
I could pump away and sound pretty good,
While my sister worked as hard as she could.
Getting the piano home was another story.
Dad found a guy with a small type lorry.
To help move it, he had three friends.
These were the times of bad economic trends.
They would move the piano for just four bucks.
Then it took four hours. This was pretty bad luck.
For a quarter an hour they broke their backs.
Trying this way and that way, stopped in their tracks.
Finally, they got it into the living room.
It still worked, fortunately. We had thought of doom.
On this old relic my sister learned to play,
While I got some exercise, pumping away.
Dad at the time made a pledge from the heart.
The only way the piano would leave would be apart.

Huckleberry Days Sequel

Contents

1. Blue Berry Picking

When we picked blue berries, I went with Dad
When I was too young, it made me sad.
I had to be old enough to wear hip boots,
And carry two pails while not tripping on roots.
Because the berries were found in the Great Swamp,
And through bogs and muck we'd have to tramp.
These berries were big like domesticated ones
They grew on the bushes, it seemed by the tons.
When I was fourteen, I was allowed to go.
I knew about getting lost from scouts, you know.
We'd get there early, and we carried a water supply.
The sun would get hot enough by and by.
I carried a compass. This was a small cost.
Coming out, it's pretty easy to get lost.
We could always get out, but we might be far
From the place where we had left the car.
The berries grew on bushes up high
With no stooping, the muck up to the thigh.
There were stories about dangerous quick sand,
But we never found any in this swampy land.
When we were little, we'd pick and eat,
But we men didn't take this tasty treat.
With a few hours picking straight through
We each filled the water pails with berries blue.
When finished, we retraced our path to the car,
And found it okay without following a star.
Then came a treat for me, a beer that's cold.
The men always had this treat I was told.
The beers were kept cold with a newspaper wrap,
Really good, but not like right out of the tap.
I had a great time on each blue berry trip.
This was an exciting apprenticeship.
Years later they tried to take this land
To make an airport rather grand.
But the environmentalists had a say,
And the swamp is now a bird sanctuary.

2. Junior High

Grandpa started junior high in the seventh grade.
This was renamed middle school in later decades.
We were there for three years it would appear,
Though it was really high school that final year.
With only seven boys from my end of town,
I knew no one in class. I was a bit down.
I think early teens tend to be a bit shy,
Which was certainly true about this guy.
School was okay, but I found on the long walk
From home to school, I could have used some talk.
I made some friends and school was fine,
Although there were problems from time to time.
This was the first time we had more than one teacher,
And we had to change classes in order to reach her.
We had lockers to store our books and stuff
Though sometimes this space was not enough.
One thing we had that might be unique.
This was the shops of which I must speak.
We had wood shop, metal shop, and some art,
Mechanical drawing, cooking, and sewing to start.
Both sexes took each of these in turn,
For six weeks, and we did learn
What we liked for a longer stint in grade eight.
Many of the guys took cooking for all they ate.
This was the first time that we had gym,
At the YMCA, though we couldn't swim.
We didn't have a lunch room or cafeteria.
We brought our lunch, eating in the class area.
Our school was rather crowded then,
But the lack of facilities didn't dishearten.

3. The New Kid

There was a new kid in class one day.
He was placed next to me without delay.
I guess he wanted to attract attention,
But I couldn't determine his intention.
Surely, he was lonely being new in class,
Not knowing a soul, not lad nor lass.
Later his actions seemed absurd,
At the time I was intent on the teachers words.
He reached over and stabbed my hand
With a pencil. Why? I didn't understand.
While I pondered, he stabbed again.
I felt rage and stood and faced him then.
I flailed the way a crazy boy would.
The teacher yelled as loud as she could.
"What are you doing? What's the meaning of this?"
My tongue was tied during this crisis.
Now there's the emotion and the pain caused tears,
But there's nothing like those of rage (not fears).
I finally got my story out.
Being known as good helped defray any doubt.
There's a lesson here. Please understand fully.
Though mild, you needn't take crap from a bully.

4. Hospital Stay

My Dads stomach ulcer got worse and worse.
Finally, the doctor was afraid that it might burst.
At the local hospital they performed the operation.
The removal of three quarters of his stomach his tribulation.
At that time hospitals had a strict rule.
No kids allowed to visit. This was cruel.
I decided to ignore their stupid idea
And sneak in anyway without making a plea.
I found a side door and climbed the stairs.
No nurse or orderly gave me any glares.
I knew the room number since Mom had told me,
And not asking anyone I found it quite boldly.
Dad didn't look so good though he was glad I came.
We talked a while, and the next day I did the same.
At home I talked to my sister, and I was glad,
Because she had also gone and visited our Dad.
Strangely enough no one seemed to care,
That two teenagers had managed to sneak in there.
Until Dad was home, we visited after school.
It took a while before he resumed a normal schedule.
Since then I realized that sometimes it's necessary to break a rule.
These rules were invented by the medical staff
For their convenience, not on our behalf.

5. The Big Snow

The big snow started. The forecast was flurries.
People went about their business without worries.
The snow deepened as time flowed past.
The weathermen never caught up with their forecasts.
Flurries when there were six inches on the ground.
Two to four with more than a foot to be found.
A total accumulation of twenty six by storm's end.
We then were free to try to contend.
This was the biggest snowfall ever in our area,
But with little wind, there was no hysteria.
We had few snow drifts. It was easy to plow,
So the effect on our town was not a big blow.
It took a while to shovel out.
There were no private plows about.
Resting from shoveling now and then
I could contemplate beauty and lighten my burden.
Life should be thus. We ought to seek
The good from what seems rather bleak,
And give our emotions a gentle tweak.

6. War's End

I know where I was when they started the war,
Listening to the radio while lying on the floor.
The formal end was not as dramatic,
Probably because it was anticlimactic.
As a family we weren't too affected I was told.
Most relatives where either too young to too old.
One older cousin had served in the merchant marine.
It was safer at the end, no U-boats to be seen.
One uncle got to Europe but saw no action,
Mostly because he was in the rear echelon faction.
But Uncle Tom had seen action in the Pacific.
This was on Guadalcanal to be specific.
We didn't know why this was done.
He certainly was too old to carry a gun.
He came home from the war with no wounds you could see,
Though he had contracted malaria, no cup of tea.
Tom had collected a few items and some swag,
Like a Japanese bayonet, some money, and a flag.
He didn't want to talk about his fight.
Like other vets, there's nothing to make it right.
Uncle Tom died not too long after that.
Malaria and alcohol had knocked him flat.
Not killed in action but a victim of that.

7. Summer Camp

Summer camp was the year's highlight for each scout.
This was definitely something I'd want to try out.
Seven dollars for each week was the cost.
Not much, but the meaning on me was not lost.
Most of the kids folks were not going to pay
Money for boys to have fun in that way.
To this great adventure our troop only sent two
We'd mix with kids whom neither of us knew.
We slept in cabins that had canvas walls.
These came down for heavy rain or squalls.
Light was provided by kerosene lamps.
This was the source of light for most of the camp.
We ate on picnic tables in a mess hall.
Whatever was served, we ate it all.
At home Mom said I was fussy with food,
And now I'd eat what was served no matter my mood.
She was right of course, since we had no choice.
Besides it was pretty good food for us boys.
We had a nature contest, and I won first prize.
This surprised me, because I wasn't that wise.
We had follow the leader, alias the obstacle race.
I was eliminated early with no loss of face.
They finished up with a mile run down a stream.
Only the oldest scouts had enough steam
To complete this exercise without falling flat,
Their leg muscles were jelly or something like that.
We had a fifteen mile hike in one day.
We all managed to finish though it wasn't play.
Only one incident marred our camp trip,
When one of the boys drowned while taking a dip.
They had stringent safety measures, this is true.
But sometimes stuff happens to me or to you.
The best laid plans of men and mice
Don't count sometimes when fate's not nice.

8. Swimming Merit Badge

I learned to swim at boy scout camp.
I could pass one test, but I was not a champ.
Swimming merit badge was required for higher rank.
This could've been too much, to be perfectly frank.
There was a scout camp ground about five miles away
Where scouts could camp overnight or for a day.
They had a pool, it was a dammed up stream.
To go there by bike was my scheme.
My old bike had balloon tires and only one speed.
So pumping up hills, some stamina I would need.
Mostly I'd get off and push the bike.
Thus, I combined a bike ride with a hike.
I learned to swim the necessary strokes, all four,
The surface dive for a pail on the pool floor,
The basic life saving techniques, and something to astound,
Enter and swim fifty feet without making a sound.
Maybe my tester was some special forces guy
Who had just left the service and wanted us to try
To do some of the stuff that they had to do.
It was a teen boy's dream that had come true.

9. Explorer Scouts

My boy scout troop had ceased to be.
I really liked scouts, and this upset me.
Then I heard that for older boys there's explorer scouts.
This was something I'd have to try out.
I went to a meeting, and a problem I found.
Fourteen was the limit. Were they rule bound?
I told the leader of my young age.
He asked if I had swimming merit badge.
I had, and this was enough for him,
Though he didn't expect we'd go for a swim.
This troop's purpose was to take canoe trips.
I had never been in one but didn't let it slip.
Thus, a big adventure began to unfold.
This new sport was great, no need to be sold.
We canoed on most of the state's streams
From the north to the pine barrens it seems.
Some trips were two day and some were one,
But the best was a ninety mile trip- great fun.
We went down part of the upper Delaware,
Where we had rapids requiring the greatest of care.
I learned all the canoeing paddle strokes,
To maneuver that boat like the expert folks.
By myself I could paddle on just one side
With the canoe moving on an arrow straight ride.
We had a great time, but then it ended
When one of us did something that offended.
We were waiting to be picked up by the river side
When the culprit took a draw bridge for a ride.
Our leader was disappointed and chagrined.
Considering all his effort, now the troop was ruined.
Thus, ended our scouts due to one who had sinned.

10. Mowing Lawns

People didn't usually hire workers by the day.
They couldn't or wouldn't spend money that way.
Though some found it hard to mow a lawn
Due to lack of will or lack of brawn.
Thus, young ones like me filled the need.
I'd mow the lawn for a price we'd agreed.
For other work the pay was by the hour
To rake, pull weeds, or water the flowers.
Since traveling to the job was by foot or bike,
The boss provided a mower or the tools I'd like.
One old guy had a big lawn and a tennis court.
He was over eighty but still played the sport.
The story was that he'd played Sweden's king.
There was a lack of old folks with enough spring.
He always gave me an iced tea to drink
And a little extra money with a wink.
When I traveled far, then on the way back
I would stop for a cold root beer and a snack.
I could afford the cost of a dime,
Having earned fifty cents or a dollar for my time.
We were always glad to work in that past age.
Now kids no longer seem willing to seek a wage.
Plus people are afraid a kid could get hurt,
And the parents would sue, they do assert.
Now professionals are all who will do this work.

11. Baby Sitting

Now and then as a teen, I baby sat.
It's mostly for my sister that I went to bat.
This was only when the kids were in bed.
I'd never have managed if they had to be fed.
Mostly, I was a body there for an emergency.
I could telephone the parents with some urgency.
With no TV I'd try to stay awake with a book,
Then walk around and give the kids a look.
I was tempted to check out the kitchen for food,
And at times eat something when in the mood.
I got in trouble for eating the brownies once.
However, they might have warned me not to be a dunce.
You shouldn't expect a teenager not to eat,
Especially while staying up late when he's beat.
When you're tired of reading and want to go to bed,
Strange things may get stuck in your head.
There was a portrait of a women on the wall.
She was in need of some color as I recall.
The lipstick was sitting right there on the shelf.
I just couldn't resist. I couldn't help myself.
The next day we received a call from the lady, irate
She was incensed. Why did I desecrate?
Mom took the call, and she heard a sound
Of the husband laughing in the background.
It wasn't a complete disaster you may agree,
Though the whole action was pretty stupid of me.
Why do kids do crazy things you couldn't imagine?
The answer as far as I'm able to give a spin,
Is there is no answer. It's just the age they're in.

12. Ode to Miss Baker

We had Miss Baker for English and that social studies stuff.
As teachers go, she was pretty darn tough.
In fact in twenty three years of my schooling,
She was the most demanding, no fooling.
Miss Baker was one whose life of dedication
Provided excellent education to many a generation.
She was single, a bit stiff, with hair of white.
She drilled us until we got everything right.
We learned a horrendous amount by memorization.
The important things that define our civilization.
Each in order, the United States' presidents,
The introduction to the Declaration of Independence,
The preamble to our beloved Constitution,
Our founding fathers tremendous contribution.
All the states and capitols of each,
Lincoln's Gettysburg Address, and the parts of speech.
I still remember the preposition list.
Miss Baker made us all persist.
I know I said that she was tough,
But she was the teacher with the right stuff,
And the best one of all. I do not bluff.

13. Bad John

John moved into the house up the street.
They took over the greenhouse where I'd worked in the heat.
They came from Pennsylvania. The dad mined coal.
To be a tough guy seemed to be John's goal.
For some reason he took an instant dislike to me.
Maybe because I was a book and homework devotee.
One day his feathers were ruffled somehow.
Who knows what caused this silly row.
"I'll meet you after school and we'll fight."
"Where?" I asked, so we'd get it right.
I had no desire to fight this lout,
But knew it wouldn't end 'til we'd had it out.
So after school I went to the designated spot.
John didn't show up, and he'd seemed so hot.
I started home and saw him up ahead
I caught up, and there wasn't any dread.
We wrestled in the mud and dirt.
John said,"Let's stop cause I'll ruin my shirt."
He didn't mind picking a fight with me,
But wouldn't suffer the consequences, thus the plea.
John and I weren't in any class together except gym.
There's where I had the only other tussle with him.
He dropped out of school along the way,
And his family couldn't make the greenhouse pay.
They moved away, and I hope he changed his life.
Being a bully just causes too much strife.
You can hurt someone really bad, a crime,
And wind up in jail serving some time.
Also, a victim could ruin your day
By retaliating with a gun and shooting away.

14. Bean Sandwiches

When people think of beans, Boston baked comes to mind.
These served with franks are good you'll find.
My family regularly had lima beans, dried.
I never came to like them however I tried.
To prepare them, soak them in water for a day.
Then cook for hours in a simmering way.
By then they're softened enough to eat.
Add a chunk of salt pork for an extra treat.
When visitors came, especially Uncle Bob,
They'd say , " Oh boy, beans," with hearts a throb.
In times of old for people of limited means,
Meat was rarely eaten and protein came from beans.
Limas when first prepared were eaten hot.
The next day eating them cold was their lot.
Saturday night was the traditional time for the bean
Maybe people wanted to go to church and be mean.
Not only did I not like beans a whole bunch,
The crowning blow was a bean sandwich for lunch.
I told Mom I wouldn't eat it, no matter what.
She made that sandwich. It wouldn't enter my gut.
I threw the offensive lunch in the trash can.
Leaving the school for a local store, my plan.
Mom mostly thought I was a fussy eater.
When I chucked my lunch, I didn't cheat her.
I know beans are called the musical fruit,
But personally I don't give a hoot.

15. Extra Credit

All through grammar school many kids did it.
We worked a little more. Call it extra credit.
We'd write several little history reports
Concerning the ancient people of all sorts.
Once a week, book reports were due.
Sometimes to stand out, we'd turn in two.
This was a competition between the guys.
We were working for marks as a prize.
At the time we didn't think this was so bad.
Being called sycophants would have made us mad.
This procedure was the same through junior high.
Then it stopped, but I'm not quite sure why.
This last extra credit was a history chore.
I made a set of miniature medieval weapons of war.
I never knew if extra work aided the grade.
Was there any effect on the impression made?
Anyway, this was one way to stand out in a crowd.
The polite way to say this is you "kowtowed."
However, to really stand out from the mass,
Just show the teacher your interested in class.

16. Wood Shop

We first had wood working shop in grade five.
We could rarely use a power tool, goodness sakes alive.
They did let us use a power jig saw.
You could cut a finger but little blood you'd draw.
The teacher cut most of the pieces for us.
Our job was to sand them and not cuss.
Our teacher put black pencil marks where
He wanted more sanding, to our despair.
I got to like working with wood in shop,
And this continued through life without stop.
I decided to buy some power tools of my own,
A small jig saw and table saw, the cheapest known.
I also bought a lathe and a grinding wheel,
Which have lasted many years, a pretty good deal.
I made little items, each used as a gift,
Such as small shelves to give Mom a lift.
My interest in woodworking has lasted my life,
Making things for my kids and for my wife.
It provided income both in summer and part time,
Both in high school and college (while in my prime).
Finally, I developed long standing ambitions
To build a house or put on additions.
I lost fear of trying and any inhibitions.

17. Cards

I have this lifelong dislike of cards.
The reason is seeing playing hazards.
My folks played with two uncles and spouses.
Normally, all got along fine with no grouses.
But when they played women against men,
Or teamed with spouses why then,
The fir would fly. No holds barred,
Make a mistake, you'd be feathered and tarred.
They played pinocle, canasta, or hearts.
I never cared which when seeing the darts
That were tossed. Fortunately, no bets allowed.
Then the players would certainly be cowed.
More than one tear was shed,
When the epithet, "You damn fool." was said.
After growing up I witnessed the same,
And wonder, why get so upset over a game?
A social occasion should be a pleasant time.
Not where a mistake is treated like a crime.

18. Youth Group

When I was young, I didn't spend time in church much.
Sometimes I went to Sunday school and such.
I managed to participate on Children's Day
And got a personal bible along the way.
They started a youth group for the teen years
Which I joined, liking to socialize with my peers.
With morals, my church didn't want to take a chance.
Therefore, no one was allowed to dance.
Since the youth group had both girls and boys,
To broaden our contact we developed some ploys.
It was decided that square dancing was okay.
It is kind of strange to think this way.
There's a lot more body contact with the prancing
Than you would ever get with ballroom dancing.
We enjoyed our socializing in this way,
As well as the talk on problems of the day.
The older guys drove us home from our meeting,
Packing us kids in a car with not enough seating
Was fun in itself. We didn't go too far.
There was no groping in the crowded car.
It was good for us with a hand to hold,
And an arm round the waist, not being too bold.
The closeness was nice. In fact it was great,
And we didn't have to ask for, or accept a date.

19. My Rifle

I wanted to buy a rifle, a twenty two.
Something simple, a single shot would do.
I found just what I wanted at the Sears store.
It was in the catalog, but then I swore.
In New Jersey they couldn't deliver a gun.
It wasn't in the store, and I wanted that one.
This was a conundrum. Could I get around it?
My Mom had an idea that was a pretty good fit.
We could have them deliver it to Aunt Sue,
Who lived up in Mass. This should do.
I managed to get my rifle in a round about way.
Maybe I flaunted the law, some would say.
I could buy ammunition in many a store,
No questions asked, when I wanted some more.
I went to the copshoot when no one was there,
And became a pretty good marksman, I do declare.
I was tempted to do something with more action.
When the target falls over, there's more satisfaction.
I took an old light bulb and mounted it out back.
I could shoot from my bedroom and give it a smack.
The next day right after I rose from bed,
I shot out back hitting the bulb as I said.
Mom didn't say anything. Maybe she hadn't heard.
So the next morning I shot. There would be no third.
The second shot Mom heard and shouted at me.
"No more shooting or that gun's history."
She was thinking of Dad, I do believe.
Who used to shoot his shotgun on New Years Eve.
The cops were waiting around the corner one year.
They swooped down. Why were they so near?
They'd known from the past, it would appear.

20. Breakfast

I decided that I should make my own breakfast.
Time was no problem for my morning repast.
I did something odd for a kid even then.
I rose at five for my homework regimen.
My desk was the family dining room table.
Eating while studying was quite understandable.
Mom didn't mind when she saw I could cook.
She then had time for the paper or a book.
My standard breakfast was three eggs at most
With some wake up juice and two pieces of toast.
Some milk, some catsup, and home made jam,
And maybe if we had it, a bit of ham.
There's something about which you may not be aware,
Active teenage boys have appetites beyond compare.
I surely was well stoked going off to school
You can't run an engine without enough fuel.

21. The Outhouse

My Dad told about the times of his youth.
They worked hard for sure, and that's the truth.
There was time for fun when they were free,
No chores or school, they could go for a spree.
Brothers and sisters, there were three of each,
A built in gang with other kids within reach.
There were times when they pulled some pranks.
Halloween was good, then you avoided the spanks.
Some were dangerous like greasing trolley tracks,
Or rolling stumps down the hill out back.
One struck me as a rather funny ruse,
Tipping over outhouses, but not while in use.
My friends and I thought we should try this fun,
Though nobody we knew nearby had one.
We walked to the neighboring county park.
To try to repeat my father's lark.
We found an outhouse with no one in sight.
We applied our strength. It was far from light.
We tipped it over, and then I learned,
There was no satisfaction that was earned.
Our "prank" was vandalism said a different way.
The juvenile delinquent line is pretty gray.
Why did we do it? I just can't say.

22. Freshman Football

For many young men there is a passage rite.
You need to prove something in your own sight.
That you can take it and be a man
Football is great for showing that you can.
It takes the place of rites of old,
Like those of Indians or ancient Greeks, I'm told.
Not all boys have this need of proof.
They grow to manhood being more aloof.
Before we started to play the game,
The old quack public health doctor came,
And gave a medical exam. I failed.
He thought that from a heart murmur I ailed.
That was cleared up with my doctor's note.
Then I faced a problem which got my goat.
There were not enough uniforms to go around.
I was out of luck, but I had always found,
That if I persisted, things would work out.
So I came to all the practices and hung about.
The first few days we exercised and ran.
None of us had been through a conditioning plan.
The morning after our first day it was plain,
None of us found we could move without pain.
In fact all my life from then until now,
I've never hurt more than this, no how.
I stuck it out since I was resolved,
And it payed off. My problem was solved.
Some guys had enough and decided to quit.
Uniforms became available for me that fit.
There's a lesson here you should be aware,
That showing up indicates you really care
Thus started a sport that I played four years,
And it helped to allay any residual fears,
That I could take it, however life veers.

23. My Friend Ed

For a large part of my youth my best friend was Ed.
We did much together as I've previously said.
Church youth group, explorers, and boy scouts.
Though he was older, it seemed to work out.
He earned his drivers license well ahead of me,
And he got two cars in a buying spree.
These were both 1931 Model A Fords.
One was a four door sedan with running boards.
The other was a coupe with a rumble seat.
They went out of style but were rather neat.
These, even at the time, were pretty old.
They were made simply, as you may have been told.
We used to take the engines apart for kicks.
We learned how they worked if they needed a fix.
We took them on trips. The old cars were fun.
A trip to New York State was a memorable one.
We were stopped by a sheriff. We felt pallid.
Ed was too young though his license was valid.
We paid a fine at the local court.
Then were shooed to the border with escort.
This was highway robbery we could plainly see,
But the practice was widely used for the fee.
This supported the local economy.
We drove together to school for a while.
Then Ed dropped out. For him school was futile.
We went our separate ways pretty much.
Then over the years, as happens, we lost touch.

24. Roddy's Car

Before he could drive Roddy bought a car.
He worked on it. It didn't have to go very far.
Roddy wasn't old enough to get his license yet,
But he could drive his car out back with no regret.
The fields had many a bush and small tree.
Driving amongst this was quite a spree.
The bumps made the ride rather hard,
With dip and rise we'd bounce a yard.
Seat belts certainly would have filled the need
To keep us from getting airborne we agreed.
That old Nash got scratches and many a dent,
But it held together wherever we went.
There were no broken springs nor flat tires in that place.
Nothing punctured the radiator or the crankcase.
That car served its purpose in its day.
When Roddy got his license, he gave it away.

25. Mr. Kandrat

Some teachers just stand out in one's mind.
They're not necessarily the best you can find.
Mr. Kandrat stood out because of his aim.
When he taught algebra, he was at the top of his game.
Students were expected to pay attention in class.
That meant no talking or acting crass.
From across the room ne could toss the chalk,
And always hit the offender who had talked.
It was the embarrassment that did the trick.
He had no problem making his rules stick.
Now, no teacher would dare to act so,
Because they'd be the target and have to go.
Kids today often don't know how to act,
And teachers have less power. That's a fact.
Mr. Kandrat also was our football coach.
He was the type guy you could always approach.
I had him for three years of football, math for one.
He was a reference for college with high school done.

26. Rare Woods

With my new machines I needed some wood.
Only the hard types for my purpose were good.
On the lathe I tried fir and soft pine.
These chipped too easily. The grain was not fine.
About the expensive hard woods I'd read.
Like mahogany, maple, and oak, both white and red.
I found a lumber mill specializing in woods rare.
I asked my father to take me there.
Maybe they had short pieces that they couldn't sell.
Would they give them to me? That would be swell.
We found the place, and I had guessed right.
We loaded up the trunk with everything in sight.
Would they run some through their planer, I did ask.
I had in mind a small shelf for my first task.
The cost would be five dollars for the work.
This seemed fair, so I didn't shirk.
Why do I relate all this to you?
It's an example of what a kind man would do
To help a kid who no one there knew.
Many times the utility of the wood was proved.
I even took it north years later when we moved.

27. The Big Tree

The edge of a hurricane hit the town.
Quite a few trees had been blown down.
Three of us decided to earn some cash.
By cutting up trees. This was rather rash.
Bill could drive, and we had some tools.
Looking back, we must have been fools.
We approached one house and made a deal.
We'd cut up and remove his big tree with zeal.
We started to work, and got it mostly cut.
How would we move it and with what?
Bill knew an old guy with a dump truck.
With this we could get the wood out with some luck.
We managed this, then our feelings did slump.
What the heck would we do with the stump?
My two friends decided they'd walk away.
With the job incomplete there would be no pay.
I was stubborn or maybe just dumb.
I would complete the job whatever may come.
The "Little Engine That Could" had nothing on me.
I worked several days and finally earned the fee.
What did I learn from being so idealistic?
Maybe, "I think I can't, " is more realistic.

28. The Grocery Store

Enough of mowing lawns, I wanted a job that's steady.
I was old enough and certainly was ready
Mom had the idea of the cabinet maker.
I liked woodwork. Mom's a mover and shaker.
There was an ad for the grocery store.
I could stock the shelves and sweep the floor.
I applied there and the storekeeper hired me.
The pay was sixty cents an hour, the normal fee.
Little did I know what then was in store.
The psycho owner got mad with every chore.
If a customer wanted something not in stock,
I'd run to the Grand Union down the block.
Keep them happy, no matter the cost.
Somewhere along the way his humanity was lost.
Put the eggs in the carton and use both hands,
With two per hand, what chance did I stand?
I'd worked there a month, then the final straw.
I knocked over a bunch of olive jars. That's my flaw.
He fired me on the spot. Out the door I was sent
Disappointed, but I thanked God as I went.
You see, the firing was no reflection on me.
I was the fourth in that month to be set free.
We learn from experiences along the way.
Working for a psycho will just bring dismay.

29. Cabinet Making

I took Mom's suggestion about where to apply.
Cabinet making would fit, and I'll tell you why.
I'd taken shop, and I liked to work with wood.
If they asked "can you," I knew I could.
I walked in and applied for a job right off,
And told the boss about shop. He didn't scoff.
He hired me for part time at minimum wage.
There was a problem. I was not the right age.
Mr. Bissell (the boss) didn't seem to mind.
I'd mostly do sanding, the orbital kind.
Mr. Bissell was British. He emigrated after the war.
He'd left everything back there when he walked out the door.
He had built cabin cruisers, then landing craft.
There were no customers, so that's why he left.
He had his bookkeeper wife, the only one.
Later I realized he considered me sort of a son.
I wouldn't be allowed to use most machines
Until I reached the legal age of eighteen.
Soon I could use the belt sander and drill.
Next came the band saw. I had reasonable skill.
The machines that could make a finger short
Waited until I was of the legal sort.
I assembled things, helped with deliveries and swept.
I learned about cabinet making. I became quite adept.
At seventeen I could drive the truck by law.
At eighteen I could use the joiner and table saw.
Mostly I worked two hours after school per day,
Plus Saturday. Summers I earned a full weeks pay.
The boss was kind and let me take time off.
For things like football and other special stuff.
This was a pretty ideal job for me.
The hours were right. My evenings were free.
Too bad more jobs like this aren't around.
Kids would learn as they earn, as I had found.
They'd be willing to build with this background.

30. First Car

I was getting older. Maybe time to buy a car.
I looked in the newspaper ads, near and far.
There was one for fifteen dollars in the next town.
I rode my bike there to get the lowdown.
It was immobile needing part of the drive train.
Lucky for me that my Dad had a large chain.
We pulled it home probably against th law.
I had no license yet. That was the flaw.
Dad took me to the junk yard for the part
Which I was able to install. That was the start.
This was a thirty six Chevy, quite neat,
A two person convertible with rumble seat.
To get it in shape, required a lot of work.
With six months until license age, I didn't shirk.
Part of the roof needed new parts of wood.
This was no problem from where I stood.
New canvas, new seat covers, new piston rings.
I probably was nuts with all these things.
I'm not the first kid biting off more than he could chew,
Working on an old car trying to make it like new.
My Dad and my sister taught me to drive.
I earned my license. My social life would thrive.
I got my car running. There were still things undone.
I drove it to school, my day in the sun.
The car was registered and insured.
To various calamities I'd be inured.
The fates it seemed had it in for me.
That bugaboo inspection had me up a tree.
They wouldn't pass it, whatever was done.
By then I'd had it with car number one.
It was classy but no longer much fun.

31. Sweet Shops

We had popular establishments in bygone years.
The sweet shops and soda fountains have no modern peers.
For kids they provided a gathering place
For the price of a "coke", we could take up some space.
The managers weren't strict in the late afternoons.
They just require that we not behave like buffoons.
Spend a little money and the booth was yours.
We could talk and joke around for hours.
For the sweet shop this was the light time of day.
They certainly didn't want us to scare people away.
After a movie we'd go there to finish a date,
And one didn't get the girl home too late.
Somehow the soda fountain has passed from the scene.
I guess they weren't making enough of the green.
So now there are no places for the meeting of teens.

32. First Dates

There's the first date, you haven't done it before,
And the first time with each girl. There may be more.
My first time out, we went to a play.
This was at the high school but not a matinee.
Taking a girl out when I had no car,
Was a bit odd, since we had to walk quite far.
I had asked her, when in a fit of bravery,
Not thinking too clearly with my body all quavery.
I would never ask Dad to drive, a requisition,
And for her folks, it seemed an imposition.
So we walked to the school on a dark night.
There was nothing along the way to give us a fright.
She didn't mind, and we walked both ways.
She even said she liked the play.
There was something that I hadn't known about.
She was going to have a party. I had a doubt
Her dancing school friends, they were an uppity clique,
Had told her this. Her house they did pick.
Of course, I was the proverbial bump on a log.
I decided my welcome was limited, the non-princely frog.
I haven't mentioned I was from the wrong side of town.
This time I felt it. My spirits were down.
So I left the party not saying goodbye.
I was a bit sad, and you can see why.
I never asked her out again, though it wasn't her fault.
Temporarily, my social life came to a halt.
Better to wait to drive for my next assault.

33. Driver's License

About driver's licenses, let me set some things straight.
The minimum age was seventeen in my state.
You had to have a permit for at least ten days,
Which you got on your birthday with no delays.
You may have practiced with sib or parent.
Ten days from your birthday, to the tester you went.
No driving school, no appointments made.
It was easy enough to make the grade.
The road test was easy. Pull away,
Drive down the road and turn when they say.
Turn around, then retrace the path.
Use the proper hand signals to avoid any wrath.
The tester would ask a few questions and give a talk.
One question was how you got there. You didn't walk.
The lecture was about safety, as you'd expect.
And your driving skills, you'd have to perfect.
All of us had to drive with a standard shift
Which required coordination, if you get my drift.
We had to have insurance, the same as now.
We could afford it, less than two weeks wages was how.
Considering our drivers ed wasn't so great,
It turned out we had a lower accident rate.

34. Football

Our school had a freshman-sophomore team.
As a freshman, actually playing was just a dream.
Then I got a surprise, for some reason.
The next year three were sent to the varsity for the season.
What did the coaches see in me? I don't know.
Maybe my work ethic had started to show.
I had always made practice. I did all the work.
When the coach said, "Do it," I didn't shirk.
My position was one of the "unskilled," a guard.
They should say "unheralded," because the job's just as hard.
Teamwork in football is the most important of all,
Because if everyone doesn't do his job, you fall.
I'd like to inject a little sidelight here.
For many positions the need for speed is clear.
I was slow of foot, but not my reactions.
I was fast enough getting into the action.
However, at the end of practice, we had a race to win.
We losers had to carry blocking dummies in.
Every practice over all the four years,
I carried a dummy, and there were no cheers.
My second year, in three games I played a bit.
Most of the time on the bench I'd sit.
The last two years made up for that.
Three shared two positions, none of us sat.
My senior year I was on the starting team.
Finally, the fruition of my dream.
Now I know people feel you're one of the elite.
This generic fame though is rather fleet.
At the end of senior year with yearbook in hand,
A female classmate of mine didn't understand,
A good student playing with that rowdy band?
The fame lasts as long as the trickle of time's sand.

35. School Dances

In our school we weren't too hip.
We didn't have dances where we could let her rip.
This was still the era of jazz and big bands.
However, we only danced holding a girl in our hands.
No jitterbugging and the modern disco type stuff.
Shuffling around with the two-step was quite enough.
We had the informal dance where you didn't have a date.
We all came separately hoping for good fate.
No one mentioned to the girls, don't stand in a big group.
We're not brave enough to approach in a fell swoop.
Boys may make believe we're big and tough.
Approaching one girl at a time is quite enough.
So the guys stand on one side of the gym.
The girls wait on the other hoping for a him.
One girl I knew was standing apart.
I went toward her with a fit and a start.
Would she dance? Why yes, thanks a lot.
We moved to the floor but danced in one spot.
My painful shyness was plain to see,
But my partner continued to dance with me.
When the music stopped, I thanked her kindly,
And speedily disappeared stumbling blindly.
Why is it so hard to act self assured?
It's not like a dance is to be endured.
The girls were probably as nervous as us.
We're both fellow humans so why the fuss.
Too bad no one tells kids to be bright.
Just take it easy. The others won't bite.
Of course, the natural tendency to be shy,
Slows down the social process, although we may try.
The raging hormones it tends to pacify.

36. The Big Dance

The junior prom was different in those days.
In some respects things were done in better ways.
The junior class put on the fancy affair,
But anyone was allowed to attend there.
The dance was in the gym freshly attired
With hand made decorations, a band was hired.
It was expected that everyone had a date.
The difference was dance cards. That wasn't so great.
Several of the dances were given a number.
Most felt that our fun, this would really encumber.
You had to fill out the card in advance.
This meant asking non-dates. Did I have a chance?
Asking one young lady would be enough of a shock.
Asking several, for a loop, I'd be knocked.
This was a formal system of old.
But it didn't take account of those left out in the cold.
One person could have a partner for a dance,
While their date was left alone, like paying penance.
Each girl had a corsage from her date and wore a long gown.
Guys wore a tux or a dark suit, blue or brown.
I asked a young lady from the sophomore class.
We didn't know each other, so it took some brass.
I filled only one other name on my dancing card.
That was enough for me. Asking was too hard.
On the date we had a pretty good time.
We doubled with a new friend of mine.
After the dance we went out to a club.
This may seem strange, but there's the rub.
They didn't mind kids, and there's no way we'd get drinks.
We had food and sodas and tried no high jinks.
This was my first foray on a really big date.
It all worked out well even lasting quite late.
In later years I've often thought back,
And wondered about my big social lack.
"Why didn't you ask her out again, you simple hack?"

37. The Second Car

All my life inspection has caused me pain.
It started the first time when it made me insane.
Whatever I did, my old car wouldn't pass.
Should I get a car with a bit more class?
Some folks get attached to inanimate objects like a car.
I've often had the opposite feeling by far.
A guy I knew had a forty one Buick for sale.
It seemed in excellent shape both hearty and hale.
Though the car looked good and ran fine,
The price, I didn't realize, was out of line.
My folks knew this, though I did not.
I was bound and determined. I didn't know a lot.
I bought the car. I was the king of the road.
It was a nice set of wheels, my spirit unbowed.
Now I could go on a date with a girl.
My social life would be a mad whirl.
It didn't work out that way of course.
At least my car wouldn't be an embarrassment source.
I was able to go on dates even double.
That fancy Buick didn't give me any trouble.
Now my folks were right in opposing my decision,
But the car lasted several years working with precision.

38. Mr. Cliver

Mechanical drawing was tried in seventh grade.
The decision to take it again was made.
Most didn't think that this was appropriate
For those who intended to graduate
With college prep. But for me it was clear,
Since I planned an engineering career.
Mr. Cliver was the teacher of each age.
From twelve to eighteen, kids at each stage.
He was a slender man and quite short,
But he made it clear. He was the tough sort.
Every class got the same story.
That he was a champion boxer exemplary.
Except for the seventh grade, all students were male.
So the story was meant to impress without fail.
To my knowledge no one ever challenged him.
They behaved in class. No trouble on a whim.
I liked Mr. Cliver and took drawing thrice.
He wasn't actually a mentor, but I took his advice.
The time in senior year, I bought a car.
Mom and Dad thought it cost too much by far.
They even asked Mr. Cliver to intervene,
So the error in my ways would be seen.
They were afraid I would mess up my college chance.
Maybe I'd accept a teacher's idea of finance.
I convinced both that college was still the plan.
No car would interfere with this young man.
I liked Mr. Cliver. He was as a teacher should be,
Fair and kind with some advice for a kid like me.

39. Traveling

With a working car we could travel some more.
Like a trip to the beach on the Jersey shore.
This was great for a double date.
When we got home, we wouldn't be late.
Ed, the second, my new found friend,
On various trips, we were a good blend.
Sometimes we'd bring food, but nothing fancy.
We'd cook on a sterno stove, the outcome not chancy.
Ed really became addicted to pineapple and spam.
Each time we had it, his mouth he'd cram.
Certainly not the height of cuisines,
But tasty enough, better than franks and beans.
Once we traveled up north to see a classmate.
She'd gone to a private school out of state.
We stopped at the school's visitors office to ask.
First, the lady there took us to task.
"Normally," she said, "Gentlemen show up in a jacket and tie."
Here were two bums who just happened to drop by.
We apologize profusely, and she gave us a chance,
And called our young friend though somewhat askance.
It was not a big deal. We talked for a while,
Then politely took our leave, not much style.
After we left, we felt kind of dumb.
We'd entered a world we were definitely not from.
We explored a bit, then started for home.
It was rather dark, so no longer we'd roam.
We found a remote spot to sleep a bit,
And were awakened with a bright light lit.
A local cop roused us with some agitation,
And asked for licences and car registration.
Then he took us to the local police station.
Since my car was in my mother's name,
We had to call home so there' would be no blame.
The cop wanted to make sure we had permission

To use the car. We satisfied his suspicion.
Next time we'd sleep at a highway truck stop,
And avoid the confrontation with a cop.
It was certainly an adventure hard to top.

40. Going Steady

I may have the record of the socially cursed.
I had the smallest ratio of second dates to first.
In plain English I took quite a few gals out once.
I lost my nerve for a repeat. What a dunce?
Or maybe I just had the innate skill
To determine who just didn't fit the bill.
All seniors took the civics course/modern history.
A young lady chose the seat right next to me.
She was able to talk quite easily,
And I found that I could respond breezily.
Never before was I able to talk with a gal
Without turning red and feeling quite foul.
Essentially, she had made herself available,
And I knew requesting a date, I wouldn't be fallible.
We started dating and were an item in school.
Going steady with a girl, I felt quite cool.
I realized why I hadn't seen her more.
She'd moved back, having lived in town before.
She'd gone to parochial school through grade eight.
So she knew many kids and needn't assimilate.
There was one problem due to our religious creeds.
She was catholic while of religion I had no need.
I always had the feeling about parents, both sets.
That they didn't approve, was a pretty good bet.
Nobody ever said anything about it though.
They probably figured it would settle out somehow.
We were steady daters for almost two years.
We enjoyed all the activities with our peers.
After high school a nursing student she became,
And I started college, Rutgers by name.
As often happens with kids' first love,
Ours broke off, maybe with help from above.
Down deep I knew that it wouldn't last,
And fortunately we naive kids hadn't acted too fast.
Another more suitable guy had arrived on the scene,
And within a short time my life returned to serene.

41. College Applications

As far as applying to college, two would do.
There was no danger of rejection I knew.
That I was a good student was one reason,
And not many kids applied in that season.
The councilors we had weren't that good.
They made up their minds as you expected they would.
"Go to Harvard." "I don't have the money."
"Go anyway." Maybe he was trying to be funny.
An Ivy League alumnus had approached me.
He thought I'd play football and go for free.
This was intriguing, so with them, my Dad and I met.
We discussed expenses beyond any scholarship I'd get.
He seemed to be pressing my poor Dad.
How much could he contribute from what he had?
I had always figured the rest I'd earn.
My folks shouldn't be burdened with financial concerns.
On the way home, I consoled my father.
I wouldn't go ivy, so there would be no bother.
I did get scholarships to both if I wanted to go,
And the one to our state school had no proviso.
Besides dear Rutgers had added a good bet.
In addition to tuition, free room rent I'd get.
So that's where I went. I never was sorry,
And I avoided the work toward any football glory.
I never regretted my decision. End of story.

42. Change

Things will change no matter our wants.
This certainly happened to most of my haunts.
The first to go was my Grandpa's farm.
The buyer of course meant to do no harm.
He kept it going for a while with no luck.
Soon the animals were all taken away by truck.
The fields were still there. Maybe he sold the hay.
Then houses filled the lots along the way.
The pond in which I fished up the road
Filled up with cattails by the load.
Grandpa's barn fared better than the one up the street.
It burned, but they saved the horses from the heat.
Most of "our" fields and "our" nearby woods
Were filled with a development- new neighborhoods.
That little pond on which we sometimes skated,
Along with the drain pipe were eradicated.
The vacant old house where we were scared
Disappeared with no trace, and no one cared.
Our scout camp, I earned my swimming badge there
Was sold off sometime. This seemed so unfair.
The crowning blow which left the biggest mark,
Interstate route Seventy Eight ran right through our park.
Years later we walked along the old trails.
Mother Nature as well as man assails.
The old orchards, the pine grove, the old nut tree
Were all gone with not a trace to see.
Which I also know will be true of me.

43. Thanks

A lot of people touched and guided my life.
Through all the good times and the occasional strife.
I missed saying thanks when I had a chance.
Maybe this poem will act as a penance.
First of all, thanks to my Mom and Dad.
You guided me but let me be my own lad.
I did some exciting things. I was free.
You helped me be all I was meant to be.
Thanks to my siblings as old as we grew.
Not only do we love, but we like each other too.
Thanks all you teachers from the earliest grades.
You made me work. Your influence won't fade.
From junior high, you were really saints,
Through high school and college, I've no complaints.
Thanks to all the employers who gave me a chance.
Some hired an untried guy without a second glance.
Thanks to all you friends throughout the years.
We've lost track of each other though we're peers.
We've drifted apart, I guess that's how it goes.
I hope life has been good to you with only soft blows.
Finally, thanks to my wife of many a decade
And kids and their spouses and the babies they've made.
I know this feeble attempt will hardly do.
Just please remember, I love all of you.

44. Inflation

In my poems I've quoted prices and wages.
This may be meaningless in modern ages.
The important thing is the ratio of the two.
How many hours does it take to earn what you do?
My first job as a kid was a quarter per hour.
This would earn a movie matinee or five candy bars.
A haircut, five sodas with refillable bottles (how strange),
Or a half pint of ice cream with a nickle change.
When I bought my first car, it was junk it's true.
The cost was 25 hours with 60 cents per hour due,
The yearly insurance had a cost outlay
That took two weeks of my minimum wage pay.
When I started college, I was making a dollar.
This cost is so far out now, it makes people holler.
A semester's tuition at my state school
Would take less than six weeks. Please don't drool.
The good old days weren't always so bright,
But for some things the prices were right.
We certainly got a better deal in my sight.

45. Smells

Smells trigger some primordial reaction.
They stimulate the memory of past action.
This is certainly true in my case.
They bring me back to the time and place.
When I smell horse or horse manure,
I remember Grandpa's farm for sure,
Or the riding stable up the street,
Where we rode on rental horses fleet.
I have the same feeling when smelling cow.
Some folks hate it. To me it's sweet somehow.
The calves and colts in Grandpa's barn so young.
Such memories brought back by the smell of dung.
Fresh turned earth somewhat like the odor of mold.
New mown hay, the memories do unfold.
The fresh cut grass smell, even when fully grown
I think of countless lawns I've mown.
The aroma that we smell no more,
Sun dried clothes from days of yore.
Even the smell of cigarette smoke,
Thoughts of my loving father invoke.
My greenhouse job seemed to have the power,
So carnations have always been my favorite flower.
The smell of axle grease and gasoline
Bring car fixing memories from my teens.
Of what I am, these smells are a big part.
They and these memories are in my head and heart.

46. That Summer

You may ask, "How was your summer?"
It was eventful, in fact it was a bummer.
More bad things happened, just about the worst.
You could say my happiness bubble burst.
First my steady girlfriend of two years
Broke up with me. I shed a few tears.
My recovery was quick. Things happen for the best.
This I could take. It was an emotional test.
Then my beloved Grandpa passed away.
We had to travel north for the funeral day.
My father had kidney stones and was in pain.
I volunteered to drive up there in the rain.
My brother sat in front, my folks in the back.
We went up the Merritt Parkway, our usual track.
The car ahead slowed, I couldn't see.
I turned my head. Then catastrophe.
We rear ended the next car in front.
My folks were okay, but Bill took the brunt.
He banged his knee and got a cut on the head.
The car was undriveable, temporarily dead.
With the help of relatives and the train.
We got to the funeral then home again.
Mom's cousin fixed the car but at a cost.
A good chunk of my summer earnings was lost.
Now concerning work, I done something dumb.
I'd quit my good job. I felt like a crumb
I took a job at a plastics factory at night.
I lasted a week. I wasn't too bright.
There were two big lessons I did find.
No future jobs that would numb the mind,
And no work involving the graveyard shift.
I quickly found a construction job which gave me a lift.
After skipping it freshman year, I'd play football again.
I left work early to join all the men

Attending football camp before school resumed.
Then after a few days, a dark cloud loomed.
There was a call, go home right away.
Somehow I knew what no one would say.
I found at home that my Dad had died.
I thought I was past it, but then I cried.
This was the culmination of a summer of woe
I learned something about life even so.
Have a positive outlook and you'll know
That you can take it and not get knocked low.
Then the icing on the cake as often they say.
One reminder I've kept to this very day.
A dead tooth resulting from my brief football foray.